Young Cathy ha killer mused, lost in scarlet cloak, lying in the peaceful haven of the cemetery, she transcended mere beauty. As planned, the scene resembled the dramatic end of any well-crafted play and he'd become the ultimate director, calling all the shots. The feeling of ascending, unparalleled power overwhelmed him, seeping into his pores. It satisfied him far better than any meal from a gourmet or the most provocative sexual encounter. At this point, neither one had any appeal compared to this new, compelling pastime.

Speculation filled the morning newspaper, while lesser beings played at being detectives. As always, the cops had kept the best details to themselves, but, still, the dramatic headlines satisfied him for now. His rabid critics should take heed—there was so much more premium entertainment to come. One must always raise the stakes, allow your production to reach a crescendo.

That was the art of performance.

Other Wild Rose Press Titles by Dianne McCartney:

Dark Venom

by

Dianne McCartney

The Elijah Black Trilogy, Book 3

Dark Venom

Cover Art by *Kim Mendoza*

The Wild Rose Press, Inc.
PO Box 708
Adams Basin, NY 14410-0708
Visit us at www.thewildrosepress.com

Publishing History
First Edition, 2022
Trade Paperback ISBN 978-1-5092-4238-2
Digital ISBN 978-1-5092-4239-9

The Elijah Black Trilogy, Book 3
Published in the United States of America

Dedication

This book is dedicated to my late father and mother-in-law, Mick and Marg, who were the best in-laws one could hope for.

And, as always, to my husband, Mitch, daughter, Colleen, and son-in-law, John.

Acknowledgments

My thanks to my wonderful editor, Ally Robertson, and the rest of the hard-working staff at The Wild Rose Press.

Chapter One

Blaring brass instruments from the band on stage tempted Detective Elijah Black to plug his ears, but he couldn't help smiling. His longtime partner, Detective Alvia Sanchez, had finally tied the knot. The couple's first dance wasn't a waltz as tradition dictates, but, instead, a rather flamboyant, prolonged booty shake he couldn't name. Still, he'd never seen her and Ray so happy. It would take a braver man than him to mention that her baby bump was starting to show.

He worked his way across the crowded room, two full glasses of champagne in hand, to where his girlfriend, Dayle, stood. As usual, she had a group of admirers around her, mostly hopeful males. She didn't go out of her way to attract attention, quite the opposite in fact. Her long legs, the sweep of dark hair, and those whisky-colored eyes beckoned, and he understood their allure all too well.

Winding through the gathered admirers, he ignored the other men's downcast expressions and handed her the celebratory drink she'd requested. As she smiled up at him, most of the men drifted away to find a more fertile hunting ground. "Thanks," she whispered, a flush coloring her cheeks. "I was starting to feel a little outnumbered."

"You're most welcome," he answered, squeezing her hand. While most women would drink in the attention from other men, she said it always made her feel like a dessert waiting to be eaten.

"Ray's mother told me I'm still too skinny." She chuckled. "She said you need to feed me more often."

"That's her Italian blood at work. She told me the same thing. It must be her turn to make the rounds and guarantee the guests are well fed." He laughed. "She keeps shoving food in Sanchez's face, saying the baby needs to eat. At birth, she might have a forty-pound bruiser to contend with." It was nice to see, though, how Ray's large, loving family had embraced his partner. Her own parents had been abusive and disinterested, but now a happy crowd of relatives encircled them with a racket of sound and, sometimes, more emotion than she was comfortable accepting. That closeness would be even more valuable when the baby arrived about four months from now. As the blaring music finally quieted to a waltz, he leaned close to Dayle's ear. "Come and dance with me."

He pulled her close, reveling in the feel of her body against his own. Her scent, a compelling mix of citrus and herbs, beckoned. All of the emotion around him made him think about the future, but he kept it to himself for now. Her first marriage had made her gun-shy. Given time, he could convince her they belonged together, but he wouldn't rush it. Patience was easy for him.

They waltzed around the community center, the only event venue that could hold so many people for an affordable price. Sighting the envious faces of the men around him, he smiled and held her tight. He had never felt the least bit territorial about a woman until she came into his life.

Bright streamers and balloons were everywhere to create a festive, colorful backdrop. All of Ray's female relatives had been cooking for a week, so plentiful and delicious food covered every flat surface. Seven or eight types of tasty pasta paired with crusty rolls sat next to huge bowls of salad with tongs sticking out of the bowls. For dessert, they'd made three huge cakes and assorted smaller bites. The aromas mixed and melded. It all smelled delicious. The free bar meant that alcohol flowed. Due to some advance planning, each family or group of friends had a designated driver to ensure the guests arrived safely home.

After he and Dayle danced, they each helped themselves to a plate of food, egged on by one of the mommas. He grinned. "I'd be three hundred pounds if I let them fill my plate." Laughing, she agreed. They found a quieter corner to eat, waving at a few other cops from the precinct as well as their favorite reporter, Pamela Clayton. Lieutenant Porter was around somewhere with his wife, too.

Elijah had just finished eating his plate of food when his cellphone rang, the tone barely recognizable with the noise surrounding them. Pointing to his phone so Dayle would understand why he was slipping away, he ventured out to the much more peaceful outside hall to be able to hear the caller. The dispatcher from his precinct gave him an address for a murder. When he hung up and turned around, he discovered Dayle had followed him out and was waiting for him, an expectant look on her face. Being an assistant district attorney meant she understood the nature of his job. Murder never took time off, especially in a big city like New York. "I'm sorry. I'm going to have to cut out."

"Don't be silly. I'll catch a lift or call a cab." She kissed him. "Be careful."

Reaching down to give her a hug, he whispered in her ear, "Just don't let any of those randy Romeos steal you away."

"Not a chance. I've already got the only Romeo I want."

He dashed in to say a hurried goodbye to the newly married couple. Sanchez swore a little until her new mother-in-law shushed her. "Don't screw up," she called teasingly as he walked away. "I won't be there to watch out for you." Hurrying out to the congested parking lot, he dodged his way around the mass of parked vehicles to his car. He could have requested one of the others go with him, but he didn't want to ruin their night. Especially when they'd just had a lot of officers out sick with the last kick of springtime flu that was going around.

The murder scene waited only a ten-minute drive away. When he arrived, a noisy crowd of onlookers had already gathered around the old church. St. Edwards had been around as long as he could remember, the dramatic granite spires stabbing the sky. Dark, stained-glass windows had mostly survived the vandals in the neighborhood by some random miracle. Two patrolmen struggled to keep nosy onlookers back as he drove in. He called the precinct to ask for more help controlling the crowds, then paused on the way past to tell his fellow officers help would be arriving soon. Finding room to park, he stepped out, stretching. One news van was already on scene, their multi-colored, fluorescent logo emblazoned on its side. More news teams as well as additional unwanted rubberneckers were sure to follow at any moment.

He ignored the shouted questions as he ducked under the yellow crime scene tape that stretched across the driveway. How could he possibly answer questions when he hadn't even seen the body? Not that he would answer them anyway. *Not yet.* Reporters could be useful at times if they were carefully managed.

Scanning the bustling scene, he spied the female victim lying faceup on the ground with dusty grass framing her body. Moving toward her, he turned to the two policemen who approached him. "Did you two find her?"

The taller man stepped forward, his neat buzz cut making him likely ex-military. "Yes. Officer Farley, Detective. My partner and I check back here every night because sometimes local kids shoot up and hide back here. We found her at 8:05 and called it in."

"Any weapon in sight?"

"No, sir. At first, we thought she might have overdosed, simply because there was no damage to the body we could see. On second look, however, there are some irregularities that merit further investigation."

"Such as?"

"Her clothes, for one thing." The other man gestured towards the victim.

Elijah stepped closer and saw what the other officer meant. Her main clothing was stereotypical for the youth in this area; dingy, holey jeans and a loose sweatshirt. The name of a local bar was on the front. But, on top of those items, she wore a flowing red cape that looked curiously out of place. It appeared to be pristine other than marks from the grass, and the lush material, possibly velvet, looked expensive. A voluminous hood contained her mop of curly blonde hair. "That is rather odd, isn't it?" he said, more to himself than to be heard. Leaning forward, he crouched beside her, his knees creaking in protest. Cupped in her hands were what appeared to be two figurines. On closer inspection, he could see one was a wolf, standing on its hind legs, a threatening look on its face. The other appeared to be a little old lady, dressed in a gingham dress and wire rim glasses.

"See what I mean, Detective? It's like that children's story."

"Yes, I agree." He turned to face the two younger men. "It's essential that we keep these details confidential. We don't need any details leaking to the press."

"Of course," Officer Farley said, his partner nodding in agreement.

Elijah hoped they weren't offended, but a reminder never hurt. "Thank you. Can you check to make sure the crowd is being contained? I called to ask for more assistance. I appreciate your help." Nodding, they moved away to join the others.

Snapping on a pair of vinyl gloves, he continued examining the unusual tableau as he waited for crime scene technicians and someone from the medical examiner's office to arrive. The victim had been dumped in between the back door of the main church building and the cemetery in the rear of the grounds. Since the long, paved driveway reached almost that far, the chances of finding tire tracks to help them trace the vehicle were very low. The killer had likely kept the car parked on the splotched, uneven asphalt. The vehicle would have blocked the view from the street. The victim had almost certainly been killed elsewhere and dumped, then posed, here. It was too busy an area not to be caught killing her in this location. That, and the oddities about her costume, meant this had been a planned murder, not carried out in a moment of passion. The level of organization at the scene signaled specific intent and a carefully chosen victim.

They would check for security cameras, but he didn't anticipate success. Vandalism was common here and half of the cameras were actually "dummies," placed to discourage crime without paying for expensive equipment.

Looking across the lot, Elijah saw signs of activity outside the taped boundaries. Both crime scene technicians and a medical examiner had arrived. He greeted Dr. Haye's new assistant, Dr. Annie Levant, with a smile. A petite five-foot-two with startling purple, curly hair, she possessed a caustic sense of humor he enjoyed. She seemed like a strange choice of co-worker for her rather staid boss, but they complemented one another. Everyone he knew liked her. Although she'd only been on the job for three months or so, she'd earned his respect at once. She had an unerring eye for detail that proved essential in her line of work. Her soaring IQ had kept her at the head of her class in university, giving her the top class mind her boss appreciated. Smart enough not to let anyone bully her, she stayed in charge despite her diminutive size.

He followed her back to the body, staying both silent and a few steps back as she completed her meticulous work. Pausing to take the liver temperature, she lifted it up to read the results in the dimming light. "Been dead about three hours, give or take."

That would make it around five thirty that evening. He certainly didn't waste any time placing her here. A churchyard was a strange place to leave a body, especially in broad daylight. Dumping a corpse nearly always took place in the dark of night. Had the killer known that addicts would be hanging around the place later? Impossible to know for sure. "Any ideas about cause of death?"

Frowning, Dr. Levant searched the area of pale skin that could be seen, finally lifting the locks of her hair and opening her collar wider. "No obvious sign of a puncture or the mark of a stun gun." Standing, she shook her head. "Might be poison or an ingested drug, but don't hold me to that. At this point, it's more a case of excluding everything else it could be, which isn't all that reliable."

"I won't, but it's helpful to know the probabilities." When she moved back to give him space to work, he searched the victim's pockets and found nothing. They both stepped back then, allowing the crime scene technicians to process the body. He used the few available minutes to scan the crowd, watching as the photographer surreptitiously took pictures of the observers. Since murderers often returned to the scene of their crime to observe the aftereffects of the mayhem they'd caused, it always paid to shoot a few panorama shots of the crowd. They usually managed to get a few surreptitious closeups as well. "Are you going to release her now?"

"Yes. The crime scene technicians are done." She stared down at the body. "You think somebody has a fixation with children's books? It seems strange, doesn't it?"

"I guess we'll eventually figure out why he chose this particular theme." They both knew with these kinds of deaths, where the murderer played games, there would rarely be just a singular victim. How long a break would they have before the next one came along?

As Levant urged the morgue attendants forward, he stepped back to allow them enough room to place the body on a gurney. They lifted her and laid her down with care. Getting her corpse settled, they zipped the body bag closed and secured everything with broad straps for safe transport. Detective Hadley had finally elected to make an appearance, so they both spoke to members of the crowd, but no one had seen anything or at least nothing they were ready to share. He directed Hadley to check out any security cameras in the area, noticing his frown of annoyance at being asked to carry out such a menial job. Get over it, Elijah thought, tired of his constant whining.

Hours later, as it approached midnight, they finally finished working the scene. He headed back to his office, knowing he still had a long day ahead of him. It was almost midnight, but there was no such thing as a nine-to-five day for homicide cops. For a few days after a murder, they worked almost around the clock. After that, they had to slow down a little out of necessity. Exhausted officers tended to make mistakes.

Thirty minutes later, hunched over the computer, he had at least been able to identify the victim. Cathy Redding, twenty-five, had been reported as missing earlier in the day. Her description matched the driver's license photograph provided, minus the flamboyant cape. Her parents had grown concerned when she hadn't arrived for a family get-together. A search of her bedroom had yielded her purse and phone which she never willingly left behind.

Elijah sighed. In an attempt to help locate her, the parents had likely obliterated anything which might provide clues. He made a note of their address. His next stop would be to give the horrible news to the parents whose lives would never be the same. He missed Sanchez, who was so much better at that kind of job than he'd ever be.

As he was getting ready to head to the Redding home, the night sergeant from the front desk called. Their victim's parents had shown up downstairs, frantic and demanding answers. Apparently, they'd seen a news flash about a body being found before he could reach them. He asked that they be escorted up to this office.

When they arrived, he saw a couple in their late forties or early fifties, their frantic eyes bouncing around the room. The man, a tall blond, the woman, a petite brunette, they sat close together after he waved them to seats and shut the door. He knew from experience that delaying the inevitable wouldn't make the terrible news any easier. Meeting their gazes, he said, "I regret to inform you that, a short while ago, two officers discovered the body of your daughter."

The wife's shrieking cries drowned out anything else he might say. Her husband clutched onto her, tears rolling down his tortured face. Elijah moved closer to the window to give them a moment to try and absorb the horrific information.

"W-what happened? I don't understand," the man stuttered. "Who would hurt my little girl?"

He turned to face them. "I don't know, sir." He

kept his voice pitched low in an effort to calm them. "Our investigation has just begun."

"Where was she found?"

"Your daughter was discovered behind a local church. Cause of death is unknown at this time. We should know more later today." He paused for a moment. "Are you affiliated with St. Edwards Church on Broad Street?"

He shook his head. "No, I know where it is, but that's about it. We've never even been inside."

"Did she suffer?" Mrs. Redding whispered, the compression of her face adding years to her appearance.

"I don't believe she did. Cathy looked as if she was sleeping when the two patrolmen found her." At this point, the fact that her body showed no signs of being battered was the only kindness he could offer them. He sat down across from them, meeting the father's somber gaze. "Has she been having any trouble that you know of?"

"What kind of trouble?" The man's eyebrows drew together.

"Anyone bothering her, old boyfriends or strangers following her?"

"Not that we're aware of," he answered. "S-she would have said something to her mother. She tells her everything about the young men she dates." The words brought a fresh round of tears.

Elijah took the woman's clammy hands in his own, absorbing her trembles. "We have an excellent team of detectives looking into this. We'll know a lot more as time goes on." Now, he looked back to the husband. "I would encourage you not to talk about the details to anyone but the police. There will be members of the

11

press waiting outside your house. Don't talk to them and just stay inside. We will post a patrolman for the first day or two to keep things under control."

"Detective Black, you said," Mr. Redding said, as if just processing his name. "Didn't you catch that crazy female killer and the cop who went rogue, too?"

"Yes, sir. Our team did."

"Then you'll catch this monster, too, right? You can't let him get away with this. She was just a child." He met his gaze, his eyes ravaged. "Promise me you'll find him and make him pay."

He couldn't, of course, promise him anything of the sort. Attempting to reassure them the best way he knew how, he spelled it out as clearly as he could. "I will do everything in my power to make this killer pay for taking your daughter's life."

"I'll hold you to it." He slumped, defeat aging his appearance as his wife began to weep again. "Was it a crime of passion, do you think?"

"No, sir. It appeared to be more intentional than that. There was a degree of planning involved." They sat in silence, out of questions for now. "I assume you took a cab?"

The father roused himself from stupor. "Yes."

"When you're ready, I'll have a patrolman drive you home. First thing tomorrow morning, with your permission, I'll come and search her room. In the meantime, please leave the door to her room closed and don't touch anything. Try to get some rest."

He sent one of their kindest patrol officers to accompany them home and stand guard for a while. They deserved that small kindness at least. Spending the rest of the night combing social media gave him a headache. Normally Sanchez's job, he had to do it until she came back from her Mexican honeymoon. It took him twice as long as she would have taken, his clumsy fingers and lack of experience slowing him down. The pictures he unearthed were of a happy young woman simply living her life. They depressed him. Her post from one site that very morning said, "It's going to be a wonderful day," with a huge smiley face. Sadly, her prediction didn't come true.

Chapter Two

By four a.m., exhaustion caught up with Elijah, and he stumbled to the off-duty room to catch a barely adequate three hours of sleep. When his cellphone alarm rang, tormenting his ears, he groaned and dragged himself out of the narrow bed. He forced himself into the confines of the casket-like shower, trying not to wonder about when it had been last cleaned. Turning the shower cold to wake himself up, he was grateful he always kept a change of clothes on hand for times like this. The bracing water did the trick, coaxing his eyes to fully open. He dressed in a fresh, white shirt and underwear, then donned his suit which had survived yesterday quite well.

Finally feeling like a human being once more, he returned to the office and made a fresh pot of strong coffee in the hopes it would jar him fully awake. Suddenly hungry, he rummaged in Sanchez's well-stocked snack drawer for some cookies or crackers to ease his rumbling stomach. The reason he remained slender was that he missed so many meals during the course of his duties. Thank goodness for that, because he never had enough time to exercise other than walking and occasionally working the weight bag in the gym.

At least partially full, he settled at his desk, ignoring the creaking complaint of his aging chair. It squealed like an angry rodent. As if Sanchez could see him in a crystal ball, she called his cellphone. After his greeting, she said, "What you got goin' on?"

He laughed. "Well, right now, I just finished raiding your snack drawer. I'm surprised you don't have an alarm on it by now."

"Have at it. I'll buy new stuff when I get back."

"You and Ray on the plane yet?"

"Nah. We're parked at the gate. The flight leaves in around thirty minutes."

He told her about the crime that had pulled him away from her wedding.

"Sounds like another psycho to add to our big bag of sick bastards."

"I'm afraid so."

"Well, don't have too much fun without me."

"I was going to say the same thing."

He heard Ray nattering in the background. "Gotta go. We're boarding."

"See you next week. Have fun."

Hanging up, he reflected on how much he enjoyed her company. He really had no inclination to work with anyone else. He didn't think she'd give up her job after the baby came. With Ray's huge family, they'd have a lot of enthusiastic babysitters. Taking a minute to text Dayle good morning, he laughed when she sent a string of kissing emojis back. She wasn't much of a morning person and that was as warm and fuzzy as the early hours got.

He paused to consider his case. What sort of a person dressed their victim up like a character in a children's book? He tried to read whatever he could on criminal profiling when he got a chance, but there was never enough free time available. Dropping the body off behind a church and laying her out gently could be seen as a gesture of remorse. Did he regret killing her? Or was it necessary to his interpretation of the story?

At this stage, there were too many damn questions and so few answers. Looking at the clock, he realized it was almost nine. He stood to stop and stretch, then headed down to the morgue. Climbing down the long steps to the entry, he wondered how the staff didn't feel off kilter working in what was basically a death dungeon, always surrounded by corpses. Sighing, he opened the door and entered. Dr. Levant was already there, watching as her assistant readied the corpse and instruments. All the stainless-steel equipment shone—it wouldn't stay that way for long. He called out a greeting as he stripped off his suit coat, hanging it up on the nearby rod.

"Good morning, Detective." Levant turned to grin at him. "Get any sleep?"

"A few hours."

She yawned. "Don't know how you guys do it. In training, I lost so much sleep that I still haven't caught up. Now that I'm working, I have to have at least six hours every night or I'm a zombie."

"In my first year in homicide, I fell asleep in my dinner half a dozen times. Eventually, you get used to it." He pulled on a green cotton gown and vinyl gloves, tugging them to fit over his large hands. When he moved to stand beside the table, he joined her. To start things off, she recorded their names, including the corpse's, then date and time. Starting her inspection with skin and teeth, she said, "I'm not seeing any signs she fought her attacker. No broken nails, no defensive bruises or gashes." She took scrapings from under the nails in the hopes a valuable clue hid there. "You can tell by the way the blood pooled she had been lying in that position on her back for a while. Hence the discoloration."

"So, she lay that way wherever she was killed, then he put her in the same position after transport?"

"Yes, probably. The dark red area on her back from pooling blood wouldn't be so dark otherwise."

Her slender hands moved down the victim's well-toned legs, one finger pointing. "She has an old knee injury, probably from playing sports. See how the knee cap's a little displaced? Otherwise, she's in good shape. Good dental care, nothing out of the ordinary there."

He watched as she did the Y incision, then cracked open the ribs to reach the organs below. Removing each one, she muttered its weight into the recorder. "Her body looks like that of a typical healthy twenty-five-year-old. No real signs of drug use or alcohol." Peering up, she said, "We'll have to hope the toxicology screens tell us the story. This is as clean as it gets. I suspect poison, something fast-acting, but we'll have to wait for verification.

"I can't smell anything," she said.

He sniffed, at a loss about what she was talking about. "Just the usual scents."

"What I mean is that, with some poisons, there is a smell that occurs after it's been in the body a while. Arsenic, for example, can leave the faint aroma of garlic behind. With cyanide, it's almonds. But I can't smell anything at all which makes me even more curious about what we'll find."

"We see mostly gun and knife wounds. I'm not as

familiar with poisons." He sighed. It would be naïve to expect an earth-shattering result that would close the case. That rarely happened, but he couldn't help hoping, anyway, especially if it meant saving some lives. Stepping away from the table, he removed his protective clothing, throwing it into a nearby receptacle. "Thanks, Doc. I guess we'll just have to wait for the bloodwork to come back."

"Where are you headed now?"

"I'm going to head to the parents' place and search her bedroom. Wish me luck."

"Always."

The walk to his car seemed to take longer than it should have. All deaths were difficult, but when it was such a young woman, it seemed so unfair to both victims and their surviving family members.

Cathy Redding's parents lived about a twenty-minute drive away from the morgue. He used the drive time to focus on things he could actually change. His lieutenant had offered him a temporary partner while Sanchez was gone, but he declined. He preferred to work alone until she returned.

When he located the correct neighborhood, he saw their home sat on a pleasant, middle-class street with small, well-kept houses and tidy lawns. Double-checking the address, he pulled in front of a neat, white ranch with black shutters. As he stepped out and locked the car, he noted the tended garden full of tidy red and yellow flowers. A long strip of them bordered the drive. He could detect their subtle scent on the breeze. Realizing that the news hounds had already moved on, he felt glad for the family. Of course, it didn't mean they wouldn't return at another time.

The musical tone of the front doorbell gave a faint, warning echo inside. After a few minutes' wait, no one answered. Elijah tried again. A moment later, the lacy front curtain lifted, and Mrs. Redding's exhausted face peered out. He lifted a hand in greeting, then heard approaching steps. The red-painted door opened with a swish, and she stepped back, out of his way, so he could enter. "I'm sorry, Detective. I thought it was the news crew bothering us again."

She waved him inside, then shut and locked the door behind him. "Please, come in." Leading the way into an open living/dining room, she paused as if unsure how to proceed. She sank down onto a chair and he followed suit. Her hands toyed with the hem of her flowered apron. "Can I get you anything to drink?" The words were said robotically as if she'd said them so many times, she couldn't make herself say anything else.

"I'm fine, thank you. Are you and your husband okay?"

She met his gaze. "He won't get out of bed. She was his favorite, you see. I know you're not supposed to choose favorites, but those two were like two peas in a pod."

"You have an older son, correct?"

She nodded. "He's flying in this afternoon. It was the first flight he could get from California."

"I hope the reporters didn't upset you too much."

She shook her head. "They're horrible, aren't they? They kept shouting questions at anyone who came near. A few of our friends gave up before they even made it to the door."

"I'm so sorry. The worst should be over now."

"Your patrolman did his best to keep things under control, but then he got called away to help with a burglary nearby. He was apologetic, but I understood. He can't just stand there all day." Huffing out a strained breath, she asked, "Have you learned anything new?"

"In a manner of speaking, I guess. I just came from the medical examiner's office. We are going to have to wait for the blood tests to come back, because there was no positive determination of cause of death."

Shock made her eyes glassy. "I don't understand what that means. You mean they can't tell how she was killed?"

"It means there was no specific manner of death detected. Dr. Levant is saying it is likely some form of poison, but that still has to be backed up by solid evidence." He met her gaze. "We'll get answers. We just need to wait for more lab work." Had the information made it better or worse for her? He couldn't tell. Perhaps a distraction would help. "With your permission, I'd like to search her room and see what I can find."

"Of course. You have free rein to do whatever you wish. Anything that might help track down her killer is fine with us." She gestured for him to follow and led the way down the hall to the back of the house. The paneled door she pushed opened with a faint creak, and he followed her inside.

The crisp, white walls were mostly covered with crowded wooden shelves bursting with trophies, photographs, and books. Her double bed had been left unmade, a bulky purple duvet kicked to one side over rumpled sheets. An older model laptop computer sat on a tiny desk in the corner. "What are the trophies for?"

he asked, trying to put the woman at ease.

"Soccer, mostly. She was quite a star in high school."

That jibed with the autopsy findings. "You said mostly. What else were they for?"

"She loved theater in high school. A few of the awards were for plays—best actress, that kind of thing." She sank down on the bed, her fingers fussing with the covers. He didn't think doing so would compromise any evidence, and it was better for him if she stayed in one place.

"We couldn't find any record of current employment. Did she have a job?"

"She used to be a nanny for a nice couple from the university. The mother was a professor. But they returned to Europe a month ago, and Cathy hadn't found a new job yet."

"What was she doing to fill her time?"

She sighed. "She spent hours every day on her laptop. That's about it besides hanging out with her friends."

"What did she enjoy doing on the computer?"

She looked confused. "Oh, games and such, I guess. I'm not very knowledgeable about that kind of thing."

Most parents weren't, so that wasn't a shock. "Do you mind if I take her laptop with me when I leave? I'll give you a receipt and make sure you get it back."

"That's fine." Today, he could have asked for the family jewels and she would have handed them over in a fog of despair.

He waded into her daughter's cluttered closet. Some things hung on hangers, others were stuffed onto shelves. Purses and other accessories jammed into every other leftover space. For the most part, she wore typical clothes for someone her age: jeans, t-shirts, and sweats. He counted nine pairs of brightly colored sneakers, each showing varying degrees of wear. In one corner were a few dresses. Three looked like party dresses, on the short and skimpy side. The others looked more sedate, like the kind of thing you might wear to church.

Coming back out into the open room, he asked, "Did your daughter keep a diary or journal?"

"Not that I know of. Not since she was much younger."

"But she used to?"

She half closed her eyes as if she was thinking. "Yes, when she was in her early teens she did. She would always hide it under a pillow or in a drawer."

He'd bet she still did keep a diary, but now kept her secrets where her parents couldn't find it. A digital journal, maybe. That was hardly rare at her age. "Did she drink alcohol or take recreational drugs?"

She shook her head. "Not really or at least not to excess. She'd mostly drink wine with her friends. To my knowledge, she never tried any drugs." Mrs. Redding stared out the window. "She was a good girl, Detective. She didn't deserve this."

"No, ma'am. Of course, she didn't." He let her sit in brewing silence as he checked out the remainder of the room. Packed drawers held more colorful clothes stuffed into every corner. Cosmetics and other feminine accessories on the dresser top had nothing to reveal. All he found under the bed were a few dust bunnies and a dog-eared romance novel with a chiseled biker on the front cover.

Before he scooped up the laptop, he pointed to a framed photograph on her dresser. Another girl, a stocky brunette, stood beside Cathy against the backdrop of a local restaurant. "Is that girl a good friend?"

She nodded. "That's Gina Galt. They've been best friends since high school."

"May I have her address?"

"Her parents live in that yellow house right across the way, but she rooms with a group of girls close to the college. I don't know her address, but I have her phone number if that helps."

Maybe the girlfriend might know something the mother didn't, especially if it involved a man. "If you could write that down for me, I'd appreciate it. I'm done in here for the time being. Just leave everything as it is for now, please, in case we need to come back."

"Of course."

Leaving the parents so they could try and get some much-needed rest, he called Gina's number and got a typical chirpy recorded greeting. He left a message for her to get back to him at her earliest convenience. As he drove uptown, Dayle called to check in, and he decided she might be able to advise him. "If you wanted to buy a red, floor-length, velvet cloak, where would you go?"

"Mrs. Claus's clothing supplier, I guess," she joked. "Why do you ask?"

"My victim was found wearing one, and it didn't go with the rest of her clothes. I'm guessing the killer selected it for her because it coordinated with some other things at the scene."

"Could it be homemade, or did it have an

identifying mark?"

"Definitely not homemade. It had a maker's label inside the collar, but apparently the company is not a well-known one."

"Was she wearing anything that matched it?"

"No, but she had two figurines clasped in her hand, a wolf and an old lady."

"That's a little weird. You mean like the children's story?"

"Exactly."

After a pause, she said, "Have you considered contacting a theatrical supply store? It might be part of a costume for the stage."

His regard for her intelligence grew. "That's a great idea. Why didn't I think of that?"

She chuckled. "Because you're a man. Let's face it, you guys know next to nothing about shopping."

"That's both sexist and absolutely true."

Laughing, she said, "I've got to run to a meeting. Let me know how your search goes."

Chapter Three

Since Elijah was only a few minutes away from the precinct, he stopped at his office and did an online search for theatrical supply stores within a ten-mile radius of the crime scene. Technically, he could do it on his phone, but he was old school. It was easier doing it here where he didn't have to squint at a little screen. He printed out a list of the top five possibilities and set out to visit them in person.

The first three options were a total waste of time, with all the clerks saying they'd never carried a cape like that and didn't know where they might go to locate one. They weren't particularly broken up about it, either. In hour three of his search, store number four ended up making all the hassle worthwhile. At first sight, he wondered if he should even waste his time going inside. Frustration added to his fatigue. This shop was smaller than the others, sandwiched in between a dry cleaner and a delicatessen. The interior looked as dark as night, and he wondered if they were really open for business, although the hours mentioned online indicated they should be at this time. Once he swung the glass door open, triggering a chime, the lights came up. It was an energy-saving move he could appreciate. As he paused to look around, he saw massive racks of colorful costumes hung on every wall with extra extended poles hanging above. The innovative store owner had made efficient use of every square inch of available space, taking advantage of every surface except the ceiling. Although a little claustrophobic, he realized this place housed double the stock the other shops had offered.

"Can I help you?" a deep, gravelly voice called from the back of the store. Elijah followed the sound until he came upon a tall, burly man with an impressive handlebar mustache and gray hair that swept with dramatic flair to his collar. He wore a deep blue velour shirt paired with slouchy, black pants. One silver earring added an extra flair.

Elijah pulled out his identification and introduced himself. The man smiled, his gleaming white teeth a testimony to good oral hygiene. "I would have pegged you as a detective from a mile away. You could have come straight from central casting." He stuck out his hand which Elijah shook. "My name is Victor Mann. I own the store. How may I assist you?"

"I was hoping you could help me with a little research." He pulled the picture of the cape out of his pocket and handed it to him. "Can you tell me if you've ever carried this cape or know anything about it? And, if not, do you know anyone who might?"

"Hang on." Reaching down below the battered wooden counter, he pulled out a magnifying glass and peered through it. "My eyes aren't as good as they used to be." He read the tag that read Swanley's with the logo of a swan, mumbling the name under his breath. Taking his time, he inspected the garment. "Well, Detective, no one has carried this cape for years, maybe as much as a decade or so. That company went out of business a long time ago. This is the first item I've seen of theirs in years." He shrugged. "There are some vintage dealers who might have carried it and still might, of course, but they don't keep the thorough kind of records that I do."

"Who would be most likely to purchase something like this? Somebody who just wanted a costume for a party?"

He shook his head. "Swanley's was actually a top-quality manufacturer. They sold strictly to the theatrical crowd. The price would be a little expensive for the average buyer."

"Can you give me an idea about how much would one of these would cost?"

"Hang on. Let's see if I can find that out for you." Moving to the other end of the counter, he tapped on the keys of a laptop computer that sat open on its surface. "I transferred all of my information to digital records years ago. It makes life so much easier, especially when you have a large inventory." He hummed as he scanned the file and, after a few moments, said, "Here we go. The last one I sold was twelve years ago. The cost was three hundred dollars."

For a few yards of cloth? Unbelievable. "Was it a local sale?" he asked, hoping for some good luck.

The store owner shook his head. "To England, actually. One of the better theater colleges. Not everyone has the budget for those kinds of purchases."

Elijah could have guessed that solving the crime wouldn't be as easy as tracing a local sale. He never got that lucky. "Did they just come in the color red?"

"No." He squinted at the screen. "It also came in blue and black, but red was the most popular color."

Raising his bushy eyebrows, he asked, "Am I allowed to ask if the cape was part of a crime scene?"

"You can ask, but I'm afraid I can't answer that."

He smiled. "I thought that's what you'd say, but I had to ask. Like a lot of people, I'm nosy by nature."

"Thanks for your help, Mr. Mann. If you keep your eye on the news, at some point, you'll get your answer."

Waving a nonchalant hand as though stirring the air, he said, "Call me Victor, Detective. Everyone does."

He shook hands. "I appreciate the help, Victor." Turning, he exited the store, his thoughts buzzing. His phone rang, disturbing the quiet as he opened the car door. "Detective Black."

"This is Gina Galt speaking. You left a message for me to call?" Her voice was shrill and sounded defensive. She probably couldn't imagine what the call was about and likely thought she might be in trouble. Innocent people always worried about talking to cops. Guilty people didn't give a damn. "Yes, Ms. Galt. Thank you for calling me back. Could I meet you somewhere to discuss something for a few minutes?"

"Why? I mean, I'll come, of course, I just wondered what all this was about."

"I'd rather speak face to face if at all possible. Are you at home?"

"No, I'm grabbin' a bite to eat before I go to work." She named the restaurant.

"Actually, I'm right around the corner from you. May I come and meet you there?" When she replied in the affirmative, he asked what kind of clothes she wore so he could pick her out from the other diners. After her startled response, he hung up and shut his car door again, locking it. By some rare piece of luck, she was only five blocks away, so he would walk instead of struggling to find a new parking place in such a congested area.

A few minutes later, he located the colorful restaurant sign with no difficulty and realized, on entering, it was a cybercafé. Kids in their teens and twenties sat staring at various devices, looking intent, and gave him a death stare when he entered. The suit he wore and his age made him unwelcome in their midst. Elijah felt like reassuring them that it wouldn't have been his choice of destination. He found the girl he searched for at a back table, her eyes narrowing as he approached. The pink scarf she'd mentioned stood out as a feminine flag. "Gina?' he asked, looking down as he paused beside her.

The short brunette wore long, chandelier earrings and bright blue glasses too big for her pale face. Her eyes darted to his as he read both curiosity and dread in her expression. "Yes. I guess you're Detective Black."

Nodding, he showed her his identification, watching as she took a careful look. "May I sit?" He gestured to the plastic chair across from her.

"Sure." She shoved her bangs out of her eyes. "Is everything okay?"

He met her gaze, wishing there was a better way to deliver heartbreaking news. "I'm afraid I have some bad news about your friend, Cathy Redding."

"Cath?" Her dark eyebrows drew together. "I just talked to her the other day. W-what happened?"

"I'm afraid she was found dead late yesterday."

Her mouth dropped open. She tried to speak, but

nothing came out except a squeak. Suddenly, she burst into tears. Gusts of wailing breath burst out, like the prelude to a tornado. The people sitting close by glared at him as if he was at fault, their eyes acting as judge and jury. He simply waited until her tears slowed and she quieted, then finished what he had to say. "Some patrol officers discovered her body in back of St. Edward's Church on Broad Street. She'd been murdered."

"B-but everyone loves her. I mean I don't know why anyone would hurt her." She rocked forward in her chair, then back again, her arms folded against her stomach as if trying to soothe herself.

"When's the last time you spoke to her?"

She bit her lip as if she spoke. "I guess it was Friday."

"What did you talk about?"

"I wanted her to go shopping with me on Saturday, but she had some kind of lame family deal."

"Do you know if she had anything planned for Friday night?"

"Jeez." She rubbed her hands over her face. "No, she said something about being bored out of her mind. She talked to a few friends on social media, I guess. That's about it."

"She didn't mention anything about going anywhere Saturday morning?"

"No."

"Was she dating anyone?"

"No. Not anymore."

"But there had been someone recently?"

Gritting her teeth, she raised one trembling hand to swipe at her face. "Yeah, this one guy, Terry, but he turned up to be a real turd. Cheated on her with one of her co-workers and wouldn't even say he was sorry."

"Do you know Terry's last name?"

"I call him Terry the Turd, but his real last name's Poletti. Thinks he's hot stuff 'cause his old man owns a restaurant. It's just some shitty dive downtown."

When asked, she told him the location of the restaurant. He wrote the information down on his pad. "Is there anyone else she's been worried about or had problems with lately?"

"Nah. Like I said, everyone likes her." The corners of her lips turned down and her voice quavered. "Liked her, I mean."

"Do you know if she still kept a diary? Her mother mentioned that she used to, but we couldn't find one anywhere."

She sighed. "Cathy didn't really want them to have access to it anymore. You know how it goes. She loved them, but they still thought she was a kid."

"I understand. Do you know where she kept it?"

"She had a file on her computer called math problems. She knew they'd never look there."

"That's good to know. Thank you."

"Do you think it'll help?"

"It's worth a look." He slid a business card across the table. "Can you call me if you think of anything else that might help?"

"Sure." She took it in both hands and studied it like a precious treasure. As he said his goodbyes and made his exit, she continued to stare at it as if doing so might bring her friend back.

He ran through everything they knew about the case on the drive back to the precinct. Having made it back to the office, he took a seat and paused to reflect. It always seemed terribly unfair when young people lost their lives—no chance to meet their love, marry, have children. *Such a waste.*

By eleven p.m., he was wiped and headed home to grab some sleep.

At the crack of dawn on Monday, Elijah was back at his desk. He worked the few clues they had. When his phone rang, he saw it was Pamela, his favorite reporter. After his case from last year, when she'd been attacked by a suspect and helped save Sanchez, they'd learned to work well together. Since they had a press meeting downstairs in an hour, he wondered why she would call now. "Hey, I thought you'd be headed my way pretty soon."

"I will be, but we just got an anonymous tip and I thought you'd better know. The information about the girl being in a costume leaked. It will be on tonight's news and I'll have to ask you about it at the briefing."

"Damn it."

"I know. I'm sorry."

"No, I'm not mad at you. I know how these things work. Was it one of your regular informants who called?"

"No. It was anonymous, and the caller used voice distortion. You know what that means."

He sighed. "It's likely the killer playing games."

"I'm afraid so. Anyway, I've got to run. I'll be asking about the costumes. I don't think any of the other reporters know yet."

"Thanks for the heads-up."

"Any time." Since he had given her a thorough interview about the Cara Belton case after it was over, she repaid him by giving him a helpful tip now and then. The news about the leak angered him, and he wondered whether it really had been the killer who called Pamela. These cases were difficult enough without a killer's constant bid for more attention.

Leaving to go to the media briefing a short while later, he pondered how to deal with the costume question. He stood in line with the mayor and commissioner until it was his turn. Baking under the lights, he pulled a hankie from his pocket and wiped sweat from his brow. When he stepped up to the microphone, Pamela stood front and center. He chose her first, figuring he might as well get her awkward question out of the way. She gave him a sympathetic smile. "A confidential informant told me that the victim was dressed in a very specific costume. Can you tell us if that's true and, if so, provide more details?"

"Yes. The victim wore a piece of clothing and carried certain items, both of which represented a tale from children's literature." He heard the hum of interest that worked through the crowd. When others shouted, "Which book?" he ignored them.

Now, he picked another man and the questions continued. "Do you think this could be a student or recent graduate because of the subject matter?"

Nothing like jumping to conclusions. "There's no reason to think that. Anyone can purchase a costume at any number of local stores."

"Do you think we have another serial killer on the loose?"

"It's dangerous to speculate on such a thing. At this point, we only have one victim that we know of. I would hope that it will end there."

"Detective Black, why do you always seem to be given the most sensational murder cases? Is there favoritism in the department?" This question came from an over-eager newcomer who had just replaced a recent retiree.

The question caused a rare flare of anger, and he kept a firm hold to temper his response. "I go wherever my lieutenant sends me. That's my job." He stepped back before he lost his temper. "That's all the questions for today." Ignoring all the shouted calls for his attention, he hurried down a side hall and through the nearest exit.

As she often did now, Pamela caught up to him on the sidewalk outside. "A little rough in there today."

He rolled his shoulders as they walked, trying to rid himself of the tension that crept up his back. "That new kid better watch how much he steps on people's toes. We both know this setup works better if we're all civil to each other instead of throwing accusations." He paused to smile at her. "Thanks for the heads-up on the leak. Much appreciated."

"You're welcome. I have no qualms about calling out a bad cop, like on that last case, but I want to support good cops like you." She grinned. Glancing at her watch, she said, "Better run. Let's all have dinner sometime before Sanchez's baby comes."

"You're on."

Walking back, he shoved the case from his mind for a few minutes to take a break. It seemed strange to him that, all of a sudden, his group of best friends were paired up. He didn't have four good friends anymore, he and Dayle were best friends with two couples. It made it easy when they went out together. Everyone had someone to take care of them. He hoped it lasted.

Chapter Four

Young Cathy had looked so beautiful in death, the killer mused, lost in recollection. Clad in her stunning scarlet cloak, lying in the peaceful haven of the cemetery, she transcended mere beauty. As planned, the scene resembled the dramatic end of any well-crafted play and he'd become the ultimate director, calling all the shots. The feeling of ascending, unparalleled power overwhelmed him, seeping into his pores. It satisfied him far better than any meal from a gourmet or the most provocative sexual encounter. At this point, neither one had any appeal compared to this new, compelling pastime.

Speculation filled the morning newspaper, while lesser beings played at being detectives. As always, the cops had kept the best details to themselves, but, still, the dramatic headlines satisfied him for now. His rabid critics should take heed—there was so much more premium entertainment to come. One must always raise the stakes, allow your production to reach a crescendo.

That was the art of performance.

****

Elijah tracked down Terry Poletti at his father's restaurant, a rather cliched Italian place in the heart of downtown. Lounging back in a chair, an unlit cigarette clutched between his fingers, he looked like every wannabe punk Elijah had met while patrolling the street in his days on the beat. Some big lug, probably his old man, stood over him, yelling. The words "lazy" and "sonofabitch" made the loudest impression, travelling across the room to his sensitive ears. Elijah stood waiting until they were done, examining the garish red and white décor slathered on every surface. The odor of watered-down tomato sauce clung to the walls.

As if he had a rearview mirror, the older man whirled towards him, his tongue poking through the gap in his tobacco-stained teeth. "Whaddya want? We ain't even open yet." He hitched up his sagging pants with one hand, running a hand through greasy, thinning hair with the other. "Shut the goddamn front door," he shouted to someone behind him.

The young woman who had led Elijah in that direction winced, shrank away, and went back to her duties. He flashed his badge. "I'm here to talk to Terry."

The man glared at the boy and leaned down to slap a few fingers against his scalp. "What kind of shit are you up to now? We need cops around here about as much as we need you."

Terry shrugged. From the faint interest in his gaze, it was apparent that he might use Elijah's quest to escape his father's anger. "Dunno, Pops." His father stalked away, cursing under his breath. The door to the kitchen slammed shut behind him, rattling in its frame.

The man-boy peered at the identification he flashed and waved him to the opposite chair with a mocking sweep of his arm. "What's up, dude?"

Rather than taking his dubious invitation to sit, he chose to face and tower over him. "I hear you are

37

acquainted with Cathy Redding. When's the last time you saw her?"

He yawned so his words came out half formed. "Three weeks, give or take."

"Did you take her out on a date?"

Rolling his eyes, he replied, "Nah, the bitch had a friggin' fit over nothin' and left me hangin' with a bad set of blue balls."

He was still young enough to think that being purposely crass might impress. *Not so much.* "And why was that?"

Smirking, he replied, "She caught me spreadin' the wealth, you know what I mean?"

Sadly, he did, but he chose to play dumb. "Not really. Would you care to explain?"

"Caught me messin' around with another piece of ass. Just a little grab and slurp but, no, she had to pitch a fit about it." He met his gaze. "I didn't do nothin' she shoulda called the cops for, though. I just told her she could leave if she didn't like it." The idiot seemed shocked that she'd done exactly that.

"So, she left and you haven't seen her since?"

"That's right."

"Do you know of anyone who gave her problems recently? Maybe a guy who followed her or made a pass at her?"

Now, a look of puzzlement toned down his bragging rhetoric. "Nah. She's real pretty, but she doesn't take any shit, you know what I mean." He glowered. "Why are you askin' all these questions about her?"

"I'm from the homicide division, Terry." He waited a few beats for the words to sink in.

The boy paled and straightened up, letting his shoes slam the linoleum. All appearance of studied cool fled. "Cath's okay, though, right?"

"I'm afraid not. Her body was discovered on Saturday night in one of the local parks. She'd been murdered."

He shook his head back and forth with frantic energy, his shocked expression suddenly betraying his youth. "No way, man. No way it's her." Shoving a hand through his hair, he repeated it several times as if spewing that mantra would bring her back.

"I'm afraid it is, Terry." Tears appeared in the corners of the young man's eyes. "Have you had any texts or calls from her recently?"

Sucking in a breath, he replied, "No. Nothing after she told me to drop dead."

Was it irony or simple coincidence that she had ended up doing that very thing? Rising, Elijah said his goodbye and left his business card on the table in front of him before making his exit.

The next two days were spent in frustration, tracking down the endless trails that frequently led nowhere. He searched the Redding girl's diary which they had found under the heading "math problems" as her friend had suggested. The only interesting emails were from a guy named Sven, but they hadn't made his identification yet. "You wouldn't think a guy with a name like that would be hard to find," he mumbled to himself.

He made a brief call to the parents, but they didn't know anyone of that name. "Maybe it's a nickname," he suggested. They still couldn't offer any help. He's the only person she discussed theater with, he thought after hanging up, so he'd keep looking.

By Wednesday night, he needed a break and went home at supper time to catch up on some sleep.

****

Thursday night, when Dayle arrived at her apartment building, she bid hello to the night doorman and strode past his stand. "Miss Stockard," he called, his bass voice carrying across the room. Turning to look back, she waited as he jogged over, a square package in hand. "A delivery service left this package for you this afternoon."

It was a small, shallow box with a wide pink ribbon, about the size of a shirt box. She took it from him, wondering who'd sent it. There was no name other than that of the delivery service. "Thanks, Jimmy." The slender man nodded and, smiling, returned to his post.

Feeling pensive, Dayle rode up in the glassed-in elevator alone, paranoia running rampart. While other women might thrill at an unexpected present, she didn't. She wasn't expecting anything and couldn't imagine who would leave a gift for her. Letting herself into the apartment, she flicked on the lights and set her briefcase down by the coffee table. She locked the door and carried the box to the kitchen counter, reaching for the small folding pen knife she kept close by to open packages. She took a moment to shake the box. Whatever lay inside weighed almost nothing, just making a gentle swish from side to side at the motion.

She slit the pretty, curling ribbon and, holding the box aloft, removed the lid with caution. Lifting the top layer of white tissue away, she discovered skimpy pink lingerie; a tiny bra and panties that were little more than a few attached strings. Her hands shook and she dropped the carton onto the granite surface, the thunk it made making her jump. Bending at the waist, she tried to suck air back into her lungs.

Oh, no. This can't be happening again. She tried to pretend it was from Elijah, but she couldn't make her theory believable. Sending such intimate things simply wasn't his style.

She hoisted herself onto the wooden bar stool, her heart thumping. Hands shaking, she grabbed her cell phone, looking up the number of someone who could give her essential information at this hour of night. Grateful that Harry answered, she said, "It's Dayle Stockard. I'm sorry to bother you. I need to know if my ex-husband was released from prison. The parole board was supposed to notify me when that happened."

Lucky for her, her acquaintance didn't complain about her call occurring at night, outside of work hours. Holding her current position meant she was awarded a few favors. "Hang on," he said. "Let me check. They should have called you." She heard the muted tapping of computer keys as he searched through the records. Suddenly, a curse sounded in the background, and her stomach dropped. He came back on the line, muttering under his breath. "I'm so sorry, Dayle. He was released three days ago. The person in charge of notifications is out on maternity leave, and it seems the notice you should have received fell through the cracks." He paused when she didn't speak. "He hasn't bothered you, has he?"

"No, but I just received a gift and I think it's from him. It's similar to something he'd sent me in the past."

"Report it to his parole officer."

She gulped back the brimming fear. "I'll do that.

Thanks for your help, Harry. I appreciate it."

After hanging up, she stood to pace back and forth, staring at the lingerie. Was she jumping the proverbial gun here? Is there anyone else who might have sent it? But it was what he'd always pressured her to wear; short, skimpy things rather than the more conservative night wear she preferred. And she hated pink. He'd implied that she was less of a woman because of it.

She wished now she'd gone to Elijah's place as he'd suggested. It worried her a little that she now preferred Elijah's home to her own. Was she getting attached too quickly? They'd been dating for months, but she had no idea of what he wanted for the future beyond their recent agreement. Spending nights at each other's houses suited her, but that didn't constitute a serious commitment, did it? Even though she had huge reservations about marriage, she knew she wanted to be with him. This growing attachment was more than she thought she'd ever feel for any man again.

Pushing the box and ribbon aside, she groaned and pulled off her high heels. Her feet throbbed, and she leaned down to rub them. She couldn't constantly run to Elijah for protection. It had taken her years to feel safe on her own again, and she enjoyed her independence. She would see him in the morning and maybe talk about it then, once she'd had time to process.

After a long, hot shower, the idea of food repelled her, and she crawled into bed, huddling under the covers. Hours later, she still lay awake, listening for any worrisome sounds that didn't belong. Wrapping her arms around her pillow, she finally drifted into a restless sleep.

Two hours later, she was wide awake again.

Groaning, she gave up and called Elijah. When he answered, his voice was crisp and alert. "Oh, good. I didn't wake you."

"No, I was just getting ready for bed. What's up?"

"Is it too late for company?"

His voice deepened, and she could sense his answering smile. "It's never too late as far as you're concerned. Do you want me to come and get you?"

"Don't be silly. I'll get the night doorman to hail a cab. I'll be there in about thirty minutes."

"I'll be waiting."

She hurried to put on some clothes, grabbing a fresh suit, blouse, and accessories for the next day. After a quick call to the front desk, she hurried downstairs to find a cab already waiting. As soon as she arrived, his front door opened. He stood framed in the lit doorway, wearing a robe and pajama pants. She felt the sudden burst of heat right to her toes. Mine, she thought with a throb of pleasure. He's all mine. Smiling, she headed to greet him.

On waking the next morning, Dayle patted the still warm sheets beside her. She couldn't help wondering where Elijah disappeared to on Friday mornings. He referred to his forty-minute weekly absence as an errand and brushed it off when she mentioned it. Showing up with coffee and bagels afterwards, he seemed to offer them as either an excuse or a reason for his absence. A private errand, obviously, but she wished he would confide in her. She wasn't worried about another woman. She just didn't want there to be any mysteries between them. No complaints, just the simple curiosity of this one thing, but she didn't want to come off as insecure.

An hour later, after they'd grabbed a bite, he dropped her off at work. The day would be spent slaving for hours over the two cases she would prosecute next week. She thrived in the courtroom, loved the endless back and forth debate of the law. It had warmed her heart when Elijah slipped in to watch her now and then, when he had time to spare.

By nightfall, fatigue crawled through every muscle. She was ready for the workweek to end. She'd finish up a few last-minute details at home or at Elijah's, but for now, she would benefit from a good night's sleep.

A few hours later, they were curled up on the couch together, but she could tell that something was on his mind. "Spill it," she said in a teasing tone. "I always know when something's bothering you."

Elijah met her gaze, his expression almost apologetic. "Will you tell me about what happened with your ex-husband? I know he attacked you, but little else."

He had been more than patient about not pursuing this subject for all these months. She sighed and dove into the story that so few people knew. "Marrying Christopher was the biggest mistake of my life. I didn't adore him as one should when you marry. He was well-spoken, well-dressed, educated, from a good family. All the things I should have wanted. I thought that would be enough." She tried to smile and knew she failed miserably. "My mother was thrilled, because he certainly looked good on paper. But I settled for a mediocre connection, because I was lonely and tired of dating."

"I can understand that. I pretty much did the same thing with my ex-wife." He put his back against the arm of the sofa to fully face her. "So, what went wrong?"

"Shortly after the marriage, he became very controlling. He had been bossy before, but nothing compared to what came afterwards." She bit her lip, feeling a nip of pain. "He told me what to wear, what to say, where I was allowed to go. I'm ashamed to say that I capitulated on almost everything to start with. I couldn't believe we were having problems so soon, and I just wanted to keep the peace."

"I assume it got worse," he prompted.

"Yes. He started searching my phone, convinced that I had a lover. Then I would catch him following me if I went anywhere without him. He didn't even want me calling my mother."

"That's textbook, isn't it, in cases like this."

She nodded. "I tried to talk to him about his paranoia, but he would say he adored me and insist that I should just do what I was told."

"When did he start hitting you?"

She was ashamed that he knew that must have happened. "I came home late from work one night and he was drunk. He accused me of sleeping with someone from work. When I refused to admit to something that had never happened, he backhanded me."

"Were you hurt?"

"More shocked than anything, but I had bruises."

"Did you report him?"

It was her greatest regret. "No. I accepted his apologies and suggested we go to counseling."

"And he refused?"

"Yes. According to him, I was the source of all our problems. He made it clear that the man was the head of the household and I should obey him without question.

I would never have married him if I knew he believed in such an antiquated way of life."

"If he wanted a slave, he missed his period in history when he could get away with that."

God, she loved this man. There were too few like him in the world. "That was my point, but expressing my feelings on that subject made things so much worse."

"He didn't like you challenging him. What happened after that?"

"The next time we had a disagreement, he shoved me to the floor and broke my arm. He lied at the emergency room and told them I had stumbled over a curb and threatened to hurt me more if I corrected his version. As soon as he went to work the following day, I moved out of our apartment." She blew out a breath, remembering her frantic escape as if it was yesterday. "I just took my clothes and a few personal items with me. I went right to the local precinct, filed a report and got a protective order for all the good it did me. He completely ignored it. I filed complaint after complaint, but it did no good."

"And he attacked you the last time at home?"

She nodded. "I was working in my new apartment with a brand-new security system in place. They found out, later, he paid the installer five thousand dollars for the entry code." She rubbed her hands over her face. "I was so stressed out, I forgot to change it to a more secure code after the installer left. So, by the time I arrived home from work, Christopher was already hiding in my closet."

"And he attacked you with a knife."

Her hand touched the scar on her abdomen through

the material of her slacks. "He said no one else would ever have me if he couldn't. I tried to fight him off after he got in the first strike, but I was quickly losing blood and almost passed out."

"Who saved you?"

"My next-door neighbor heard me scream and called the police. Luckily, they were close by. They rushed in and subdued him just before he finished me off. It took three officers to do it." In the silence after her words, she saw a rare emotion cross his face. *Rage.* He schooled it away mere moments later, and she appreciated his strength in not going on a rant. "I was incredibly lucky, although it didn't seem that way at the time."

"I hate that you suffered such appalling treatment. I would give anything to take the memories of that experience away."

Leaning over, she squeezed his hand. "I was borderline hysterical for a long while afterwards, but then I pulled myself together. For a long time, I did nothing but work, eat, and sleep. Anything to keep my mind off that day."

"That's why you wanted to help with the battered women's shelter."

"Exactly."

He kissed the back of her hand and met her gaze, his eyes warm and loving. "I want you to move in with me." When she didn't answer immediately, he continued. "If you need some time to think—"

"Yes."

A smile spread across his face. "Yes?"

"Absolutely. When?"

"How about next weekend?"

An excited breath gushed out of her. "So soon? Oh, wow. I guess we're doing this." It occurred to her that she should tell him about the lingerie, but she didn't want to spoil the mood. She'd fill him in later.

He leaned in to kiss her cheek. "Start with a suitcase tomorrow, and we'll make arrangements to move the rest of your things. We can rent a trailer. I know Seth and Ray would help with moving the furniture. We'll have to get creative on how to fit it all in."

She knew the furniture she owned wouldn't mix with this home. "Do you want to hear the truth? I like these antiques so much better than my stuff. Why don't I sell it all?"

"Are you sure?"

"Yes. The furniture's in great shape, so I shouldn't have a problem getting rid of it. I have one favorite chair I'd like to bring. I won't miss the rest." She narrowed her eyes in mock warning. "I do have a warehouse full of clothes, though, so be prepared."

"There's a lot of room for both of us." He paused. "There's something else I'd like you to think about. I'd like to meet your mom and step-dad in the near future. Is that okay with you?"

She loved that he was traditional enough to think of such things. "Of course. We could either fly up there or have them here for a short trip. Which do you think would be best?"

"I'd say with our workloads, having them come here would be the better bet, don't you? Maybe bring them in for a long weekend, and they can stay here with us." He frowned. "It might be wise to warn them that I'm bound to get called away at some point. I don't want them to think I'm rude or thoughtless."

"You worry too much. They're used to my schedule. They'll be really excited to come, and they're good at taking care of themselves if need be."

After they were in agreement about the plans, they celebrated, as couples do, until the wee hours of the morning. The future plans seemed to have inspired Elijah in a whole new way. In the morning, she couldn't wipe the smile off her face.

****

Elijah woke first in the morning and watched her face as she slept. The truth is, if he had his way, he would ask Dayle to marry him tomorrow. After giving it some thought, though, he realized her fears about marriage were much deeper than his. And who could blame her, considering how her first marriage had worked out. Moving in first on a trial basis would reassure her that they could live together peacefully. He had no doubts. But he wanted her to be in the same position.

He did wonder, however, how her mother would feel about them living together without benefit of a marriage license. That was the reason for the suggested trip. He wanted to have a quiet word with both of them about his intentions and how he was trying to allay her fears. He knew little about them, but, hopefully, after a visit, they would all be as excited as he was about the future.

Chapter Five

After Dayle woke and showered, she appeared distracted. They grabbed a quick breakfast and settled in the car. She immediately started fiddling, her hands in her lap. "Are you okay?"

"Fine." She smiled to reassure him, but he could see the dark circles under her eyes.

"Did you sleep well?"

"Not so much."

He leaned over to stroke her hand. "What can I change to make you more comfortable? After all, it's our place now."

"My brain just wouldn't shut down. I like bouncing my problems off you, because I value your perspective. I seem to run to you for everything, though, which isn't fair."

"Is anything wrong? You seem tense." *She's not getting cold feet, is she?*

"Let's talk about it tonight. What are we building at the shelter today?" Their work at the shelter that cared for abused families gave him a sense of purpose, as it did her. Volunteer work always gave one a sense of community. The fact that he had donated a chunk of money to the cause was just icing on the cake.

He'd let her change the subject, for now, but he would get to the bottom of her concerns. "The kitchen table and some extra storage. Seth has the wood and everything cut, so it shouldn't take long to nail or screw it together." He smiled. "I asked Pamela Clayton to come by."

She chuckled. "I like her, but I can't see her doing much manual labor. She might break a nail."

"My purpose is two-fold," he explained. "She said she might be able to drum up some local support for the shelter, but I also thought she and Seth might get along."

His comment surprised her. Raising an eyebrow, she said, "Funny, you don't look like a stereotypical matchmaker."

He fidgeted at her use of the term. "It sounds strange, but I think they're both a little lonely and they are each other's type. Apparently, he's into smart blondes and she wants a nice, good-looking guy who knows how to treat a woman. It can't hurt to try, right?"

"That's probably true, but I guess the potential success of it remains to be seen."

When they parked, they saw their early-bird friend, Seth, waiting by his truck, standing propped against the bumper. Dressed in faded jeans paired with a blue and black checkered shirt, he was drinking from his usual to-go cup of coffee. "Good morning," he called as they walked over. "Ready for some hard work?"

Elijah looked at the pile of lumber in the bed of his truck, beautifully planed and already notched for fitting. The scent of fresh hewn wood lingered in the air around them. "Yes, this looks great. Let's get started."

"How can I help?" Dayle asked.

Elijah scanned the load. "You can carry the small pieces. Leave the large ones for us."

They found Sara waiting inside and were surprised to see Pamela had already arrived. The men put down their load of lumber in a corner of the kitchen and Elijah introduced Seth to Pamela. They shook hands and he almost chuckled at the interested gleam in Seth's eyes. "Do you guys mind if I take pictures as you work?" she asked. "I thought we might post them for some social media exposure."

"Sure. Just don't list the address for the sake of security."

"Yes, Sara told me. We just list a place where people can donate if they want."

The three of them made multiple trips back and forth while she shot photographs and spoke to Sara. Elijah didn't miss the fact that Pamela's eager gaze kept drifting to Seth. When they started hammering the pieces together, he was impressed how neatly the notches fit. "This is really nice, Seth. You know your stuff."

"Thanks." He grinned. "I had fun picturing all the kids who could pile on it."

It took about ninety minutes to put the pieces together. While Seth worked on the finishing touches, Elijah talked to Sara. "Were you able to track down all the appliances you want for the kitchen?"

She laughed. "I was holding out for a better deal from the supplier, and he came through for me. He gave us an extra fifteen percent off. They should be here by Wednesday."

"That's wonderful news."

When they finished tidying up the work site, they said goodbye to Sara and left her to show their work off to the residents, who seemed excited. Elijah proposed that the four of them grab some brunch before they went their separate ways. They met at a local pancake house. Despite the plain Jane exterior, it boasted excellent, cheap food. It didn't miss his notice that Seth pulled Pamela's chair out for her and sat as close as he comfortably could. She turned to him, smiling. "I heard you're writing your detective's exam next week."

"Yes. If you can cross your fingers, wish on a star, or pray to any entity, I'd appreciate the good karma."

"What division do you hope to work in?"

"Homicide, eventually, but that's kind of the holy grail, isn't it? You have to prove yourself in another less-demanding division first."

"What's wrong with us?" she teased. "We all clamor to follow death and destruction in one form or another."

They looked at the menus and all chose plain pancakes with maple syrup and bacon. "I'm glad you ladies aren't the type to pick a little dish of fruit and call it a meal," Seth said. "You must both work out."

"I like to work out a few times a week. It certainly helps. How about you?"

"The same. Usually, three times a week and I run a bit, too."

Elijah let the two of them carry the conversation and noticed Dayle still seemed distracted. She ate in silence and pushed her plate away when she'd only eaten half her serving. The other two decided to go home and change to go for a run together. It appeared that his plan for them to meet had worked out well at least in the near future.

He picked up the bill, waving away their protests, and they parted ways outside on the sidewalk. He and

Dayle headed towards the car. "Your plan appears to have worked. They seem to get along."

"Two nice people. Maybe they'll fit well. Who knows?" He held her door open and waited until she slid inside. Closing it behind her, he went around to get behind the wheel, slamming the door behind him. "I have to go to work for the rest of the day, following some leads. Where do you want to go?"

"Do you mind if I grab some files from my place and work at yours?"

"Of course not, as long as you remember to start bringing some of your things with you. Make yourself at home. It's your place, now, too."

They made the rounds, and he saw her safely into his house. Driving to the precinct afterwards, he worried that something serious was on her mind. Her actions were jittery instead of her normal calm, so he hoped she wasn't changing her mind about moving in. He would get her to talk and they could figure it out together.

He chased down a dozen small leads, but none of them led anywhere. At six thirty he'd had enough and texted Dayle.

—What do you want for dinner?—

—All taken care of. Just come home—

Home, such a nice word. Especially because she was the one using it. Pleasantly surprised, he drove to the house, wondering whether she'd ordered in or cooked. His house seemed like even more of a home with Dayle in it. He'd have to give some more serious thought about their future together. He got his answer about their meal walking in the door, the rich aroma of roast beef drifting out. Raising his voice, he called out,

"That smells amazing." Slipping off his coat, he dropped it on the back of a chair.

She stepped out of the kitchen, an old, flowered apron of his mother's tied over her blouse and slacks. "Don't get too excited until you try it. It's a new recipe."

He couldn't help thinking about how much her mother would have approved of his choice of girlfriend. "I'm sure it will taste wonderful." He kissed her. "Bad food never smells this good."

Since she seemed happier now, he left his questions until later. He leaned over the far side of the kitchen counter. She smiled. "I'm getting ready to mash the potatoes. Can you carve the roast?"

"Of course." He grabbed a platter and his best carving knife. In no time at all, their plates were full of beef and potatoes along with a mound of corn. She waved to the dining room where the table had been set. A crisp white linen tablecloth framed china, silverware and glass.

"This is really nice to come home to. Thank-you for all the hard work." He dropped a kiss on her cheek before they both sat. "You're going to spoil me."

"You deserve it. A domestic goddess I'm not, but I think this turned out okay. We'll see."

One bite proved the roast tasted nice and tender, so he didn't have to fake enthusiasm. And he would have, because anyone who was nice enough to cook for him deserved appreciation, regardless. "Delicious."

They talked about their day in between bites and finished the meal with a nice, light raspberry gelato for dessert. After the dirty dishes were stacked in the dishwasher, they relaxed on the sofa. He met her gaze, seeing that she still looked a little solemn. Reaching out, he took her hand. "Are you going to tell me what's wrong? You seemed a little agitated earlier."

She sighed. "I swear you have a crystal ball. You can always tell when I'm upset." Telling him about her unexpected present led to other questions.

"Why didn't you tell me last night?"

"I didn't want to ruin the moment."

"Are you confident it's him?"

She shrugged. "It's exactly what he used to pressure me to wear all the time—skimpy and pink. I hate both of those things."

"We might be able to track him through the delivery service."

"I tried. They said a woman dropped it off at the service and she paid cash. Probably someone he smooth-talked into doing it for him. He uses people any way he can without any thought to the consequences."

He kissed the back of her hand. "You'll be safer here. He has no way to connect us."

"Unless he's watching."

"Have you noticed anyone following you?"

"No." She rubbed her eyes as fatigue set in. "I don't want to put you in any danger. Just the possibility of him hurting you makes me ill."

"Don't worry about me. I have the top shooting score in my department, and I used to do mixed martial arts." He grinned, trying to lighten the mood. "I'm no kung fu killer, but I get by."

"Why didn't I know that? That may make you even sexier than you already are."

"You never asked." He smiled. "I can take care of both of us. Do you want to file an official report?"

"What, and tell them I think some dangerous ex-con gave me lingerie? I'd get laughed out of the precinct. No one really understands how stalkers work unless you've been unfortunate enough to be involved with one."

He encouraged her to turn her body away from him and he began to rub her shoulders, feeling the tension that tightened the muscles there.

She sucked in a breath. "When he attacked me that final time, he kept saying, 'You're going to die tonight, bitch. No one cares enough to save you.' I still hear that in my dreams."

He wrapped his arms around her, pulling her against his chest. Her heart beat against him, the rhythm thumping faster than it should. "I'm right here and I care enough to save you. More than enough."

She brushed her tears away with the back of her hand. "You already saved me from one crazy bastard."

"And I'd save you from a dozen more if that's what it takes." He stroked her hair back. "Let me or someone else escort you to and from work for the next little while. That will be much easier now."

"I'll think about it."

"That's all I can ask." Turning her, he kissed her softly on the lips. "Let's go to bed. Maybe I need to remind you why no other man is going to harm you."

They went upstairs. In the shower, she marveled about how he always knew the right thing to say to her. And do to her, for that matter. Trust was hard for her, but he made it easy. She stood as he rubbed shampoo into her hair, his fingers gently massaging her scalp. After rinsing, he started working soapy lather over her body, his hands gliding over her buttocks. When they were both finished, he wrapped her in a towel and dried her hair. She felt loved and pampered as he led her to bed.

After a leisurely brunch the next morning, they worked on either end of the dining room table, absorbed in their work. Other than the soft tap of laptop keys and the outside murmur of traffic and kids playing, silence reigned. She wondered at how relaxed she felt. She'd always been the type to work alone, but it felt natural to work alongside him even if they didn't speak. By late afternoon, she shut her computer, stood and stretched. Smiling, he copied her. They ordered takeout and chose an old comedy movie to watch before bed.

****

Early Monday morning, Christopher Ferras watched from across the street as his wife, Dayle, entered her place of work. She might think a slip of paper from some legal entity made her an ex-wife, but he'd prove her wrong. He owned her. He had ever since he slipped that elaborate diamond ring on her finger. Until death do us part and all that jazz. The prolonged stint in prison was an aberration that simply delayed the inevitable reunion. Envisioning how she must have felt when she opened the lingerie made him smile in anticipation of the future.

He paused to admire his reflection in a store's plate glass window. The subtle streaks of silver through the dark blond waves of his hair added an air of sophistication to his look. Like good wine, he just kept getting better and better with age. He wouldn't repeat the careless mistakes of the past.

Having a generous supply of family money meant he walked out of prison and right into a great apartment along with his choice of a new sportscar. No halfway houses for him, groveling with the ex-cons who'd been his sole companions for years. Now, he had the added luxury of making plans for the future, plans that included Dayle. What she didn't seem to understand was that she didn't get to decide when to walk away. During all of his years inside the so-called big house, he managed to hold onto the memory of the feel of her satin skin and her delicate scent. The potential of having her crushed beneath him, begging for mercy, fueled his ravenous hunger.

When he'd knifed her in a fit of anger all those years ago, it had been a gross error in judgement on his part. Giving in to his fury had cost him dearly. Inside, he had learned the long-lasting merits of discipline. While other inmates had rolled in the gutter, he had worked on what was now his ferociously strong body. He had listened to what every fellow prisoner had to say about what they had done wrong that got them captured, using the information to devise a foolproof plan which would keep his wife chained to his side forever.

The first task on his lengthy agenda was to identify the tall, dark-haired man who often dropped her off at her office door. He would learn everything about him, including how best to scare him away from his beloved. Whoever this interloper was, he hadn't been in Dayle's life for long. The ex-con he'd paid to check on her for him had said she wasn't seeing anyone and that hadn't been more than six months ago.

When he knew everything about his so-called competition, it would be easy to determine the most efficient approach to take. Removing him from her life would be easy, a simple precursor to the pleasure of controlling Dayle once more.

Chapter Six

Elijah stole a few precious minutes off from working his case to call the warden at the prison from which Dayle's husband had been released. He was told that Christopher Ferras had been released early for good behavior.

Give me a break. He'd begun to hate that phrase, had heard it all before, ad nauseum. So-called good behavior was just a better smokescreen to hide behind. When he asked the warden how Ferras had spent most of his time inside, he said that he worked out a lot in the gymnasium and had gained an impressive amount of muscle. Some digging provided a before picture of a slick, arrogant blond man with an arrogant lift to his chin, one who, on his arrest, had been totally unapologetic about his behavior. He committed the man's face and the information about his new build to memory.

Dayle's entitled ex-husband came from a rich family, one who would likely set him up to start the whole cycle all over again. They'd been embedded in the New York City landscape for generations. Chronic enabling—it was an old, tired story he'd heard many times in the past. There was little doubt the family blamed Dayle for his problems, which was delusional thinking at its best.

What a mess. He would just have to keep a watchful eye on her and hope that she would get used to having people around who would protect her. He wanted to keep her with him permanently. That was a discussion that should happen before long. He hoped moving in would be a nonthreatening middle step.

With a sigh, he got back to work.

****

Dayle left her growing pile of work at her office by six o'clock, an early hour for her. She simply couldn't concentrate for a moment longer. Her mind buzzed with a dozen different concerns on the cab drive home. Relieved to be heading back to the calm surrounding Elijah's place, she felt like a scaredy cat. She would have to start thinking of it as their place now.

Denying her fears didn't help. She just kept looking anxiously over her shoulder and wondering if Christopher lurked in the shadows behind her. Scanning the crowd, she couldn't see any sign of her dreaded ex-husband.

Elijah had said he would bring dinner home by eight, so she would get into comfortable yoga pants and a t-shirt to work on a few files until his arrival. He had said to go ahead and make use of his office. She did, enjoying the gentle warmth of the antiques. The surrounding books hugged her like a blanket. Enjoying the combination of cozy and quiet, she got to work.

About seven thirty, after chopping down her massive stack of paperwork, she'd had more than enough legalese for the day and began to pack up her things. Pulling the desk drawers open, she searched for a stapler. The third drawer contained a single piece of luxury notepaper, neatly folded. For some reason, it beckoned to her. She picked it up, feeling guilty about her nosy instinct. Unable to resist, she opened it. It read:

Dear Elijah,

If you are reading this, I have finished my journey to what I hope is a better world. I want you to know that this mess is not your fault. You were never meant to save me, but to be a witness to both my life and death, to my story as a whole.

Being part of the wind that swirls around your face every day is much better than being stuck in a cage.

And now, to business. I left you my money for two reasons: to enjoy and to find a way to help other children who have suffered the abuse I did. I put all my trust in your ability to discern which avenues would help the most victims.

I'd say a 50/50 split would be a fair distribution. That way, you can have what you need and enjoy in life without worrying about it and still be able to administer the other half of the money to appropriate projects for my cause.

I can't imagine more trusted hands in which to leave this bequest.

And so, goodbye, my one true friend.

I'll hold you in my heart

Forever

Cara

Dayle set the note back where she found it, embarrassed that she'd given in to curiosity and read it which was a breach of privacy. She'd heard about Cara Belton, the female serial killer who'd committed what they call in their business suicide by cop. Elijah had been called to a house where she'd barricaded herself inside after committing her final murder, that of a local judge. They spoke for a few moments in which he'd tried to get her to give herself up. After their conversation, she'd picked up a gun and walked purposely into the line of fire. The gun was later found to be empty, something Elijah had warned the SWAT team would be true and they'd ignored. A woman in her department had been quick to fill her in about the case after she'd arrived shortly after it happened.

As demonstrated in this letter, their relationship was closer than she'd imagined. The pointed words sounded affectionate, almost loving. Had they loved each other? Could someone as true blue as Elijah love a killer?

Gossip around the office had told her that he had taken almost two weeks off after her death. Those that didn't like him had referred to him as a nut because of it, remarks caused by jealousy about his popularity as far as she could tell. He had told her himself that he rarely took many vacation days and that he planned to break that habit. She hoped that meant he was considering a more serious future with her.

Of course, now, she wished she'd never read the note. It was her own fault, but she worried that he still missed Cara and wasn't ready to fully commit himself to her. As she sat there, fretting, she heard the front door open.

"Dayle?" His deep voice echoed up the stairwell.

She leapt up from the chair, stuffing her papers into her case and closing the drawer. "I'm up here." After a pause, the heavy tread of his ascending steps sounded on the stairs and she went to meet him in the hall.

He leaned over to kiss her. "I brought your favorite

chicken salad sandwiches and brownies. They're sitting on the kitchen counter."

"Oh, thank you. That sounds delicious." She followed him into his bedroom and set her briefcase in one corner.

He swiveled to look at her, loosening his tie. "You okay? Nothing else happened, did it?"

She shook her head. "I feel like I'm hiding out here. I'm probably worried about nothing."

"I don't think so. From what I can see, you have excellent instincts, and you should listen to them." He slid off his jacket. "Let me get into some sweats and we can eat. I'm starving."

A few minutes later, they were cuddled up on the couch, eating dinner. She curled in one corner, and he sat propped in the opposite, playing footsies as they ate. It was a little unnerving to realize how comfortable she was spending time with him. Her shoulders finally started to relax, and she managed to eat most of the generous sandwich. After they ate, they switched on an old vintage comedy show. The inherent laughter lightened her mood, and she finally relaxed. By ten o'clock, they were both yawning and retired for the night. When Elijah's arm reached around to hold her as they slept, she wondered why she had to overthink everything. Sometimes she should just let things be simple. Far better to enjoy what they shared right now and leave the troublesome questions for another time.

****

When Christopher discovered Dayle's lover was a cop, he didn't know whether to laugh out loud or punch someone. A regular beat cop would have been a joke to deal with, but the city's favorite detective might be a challenge. But he liked challenges. How tough could he possibly be when he spent half his time in front of television cameras?

Seeing her carrying a piece of luggage gave him a start, but it was just one small suitcase. He knew his woman. She'd never move in without the benefit of a wedding ring. He'd learned that the hard way. Years ago, she'd made him jump through hoops for just a kiss. She was so square, she had corners.

It was time to find out a little more about his rival for Dayle's affections.

That night, he dug through mountains of social media, only to find this idiot cop didn't have any sites anywhere. In this day and age, how was that possible? The only thing he found was an endless collection of newsclips, portraying him as a hero. It was enough to make anyone ill.

He poured himself a big glass of whisky, gulping it down. It burned down his throat. Now, he had one puzzle to solve—how to knock Detective Wonderful off his lofty perch so he could reclaim his wife.

****

When a triumphant Sanchez returned to work after her honeymoon, she sported a glowing tan. "Now I'm dark brown instead of medium brown," she bragged, twirling around as she rubbed her more noticeable baby bump. The guys razzed her, earning themselves an enthusiastic middle finger, but Elijah thought it quite entertaining to see her in full-blown momma mode. "Did you enjoy the trip?" he asked, deciding to give her a break from the teasing.

"Yeah. I slept like ten hours a day and lay on the beach, drinking margaritas."

At his raised brow, she snorted a laugh. "Ah, chill out. Just kidding. I took the virgin option—no alcohol for bambina. But we ate a lot and fooled around all day, so it was perfect."

"I missed you."

Leaning over, she messed up his hair. "Me, too, ya big nerd. What did I miss?" He filled her in on the case and on Dayle's problem, adding that she was moving in. Shock raised her eyebrows. "Jeez. You're supposed to hold off on the juicy stuff until I'm around to hear it. What's the deal? Is this permanent or is it just so you can watch out for her?"

"Permanent."

"Well, good for you, livin' in sin. That's about as exciting as you'll ever get. You just ruined the sweaty dreams of about a dozen women, you know."

Laughing, he thankfully handed off the computer research to her, and they started their day. Just before noon, she unearthed something and waved him over. "Our victim has a hidden file of emails from someone named Svengali. Remember, we wondered who Sven was?" She frowned. "Doesn't Svengali mean a boss or something?"

"It means someone who has an evil power over someone else."

"Well, this might be something, then. The conversations are all about influencing people with theater. This one says the director should be seen as a divine god who guides you to your ultimate destination."

The words raised the hair on his arms. "The ultimate destination being death?"

"I'm not sure. Could be. Although I doubt Cathy

Redding saw it that way or she would have freaked out and told someone, wouldn't she?"

"Put everything else aside and concentrate on those emails. This is the first thing we've come across that feels like the right path to follow."

****

Elijah's cell phone rang at three a.m. the next morning, the shrill peal splitting the silence. Stifling a groan, he reached over Dayle to grab it before it woke her. Dispatch rattled off the address of a murder. "Thirty minutes," he responded and slipped out of bed, his ankles cracking in protest.

He grabbed a quick, cool shower with the door closed to wake himself up and let her sleep. His plan didn't work as well as he hoped, because when he emerged, she lay with her eyes blinking open, watching him. "Another murder?"

"I'm afraid so. Go back to sleep." Leaning down, he brushed his lips against her cheek. "I'll see you later tonight." She closed her eyes, snuggling up as she murmured goodbye. By the time he got dressed, she'd fallen back asleep. He took one last, longing look at her and left, closing the door quietly behind him.

The murder scene was close to Sanchez's place, and she texted that she'd meet him there. His car pulled up as she walked towards the line of tape, so she paused and waited for him to join her. He hurried across to where she stood. "Ray walk you over?"

"Yup. He's a worry wart."

They nodded at the beat cop standing guard and slipped under the tape. As they approached, snapping on their latex gloves, he recognized Seth Parker and his partner standing guard. "Hey, Seth. What have we got?"

"Female, early twenties, seems to be a match for your previous crime." He beckoned them closer. The young woman lay slumped against the peeling, green dumpster, a riot of blonde curls tangled around her face. Sanchez dropped down to balance over her heels. "It's a wig."

"How can you tell?"

"I can see a few dark hairs peeking out from underneath."

They stood back and watched as Dr. Levant and the crime scene team carried out their responsibilities. "Dead about two hours," the assistant medical examiner said, looking at the liver probe. "That doesn't leave him much time to trap her, kill her, and get her here. He's cutting it close. No signs of trauma, so likely poison or something similar again, but we'll see."

"When can you fit her autopsy into your schedule?"

She sighed. "Since she's the second in a series, we'll prioritize it. Let's try for right after lunch. I'll text you and confirm."

"Appreciate it." Before the morgue technicians removed the body, they took a closer look at the victim and searched her pockets. She had no identification on her. Her hair was, indeed, a dark brown underneath the wig. Her clothes looked as if they belonged on a country girl—a cotton checked blouse and a jean skirt. Three different-sized stuffed bears were tucked under one arm. A white plastic bowl of congealing oatmeal sat beside her.

"Jeez," Sanchez muttered, shaking her head. "Even I remember this story. The kid breaks into the bears' house, remember? Half of the damn book is about the temperature of her cereal."

"Yes," Elijah replied. "Apparently, this guy's on a roll. Why do you think he's inspired by children's books?"

"I wish I knew," Seth replied. "No offense, but I'm glad this is your case, not mine."

They stood back and allowed the attendants to take the body away, wincing as people raised their cameras to take a picture. *Damn ghouls.*

Talking to the group of people standing nearby, watching, yielded nothing but an offensive obsession with death. Most of them had just heard the unusual commotion and wandered over to see what was happening, then stayed to watch the scene play out. At least the retail location might yield some working security cameras, but they couldn't check that for a few hours.

A quick check with missing persons had yielded a possible identity that would have to be confirmed. Katy Byzinski, a twenty-six-year-old waitress, had failed to show up for her job yesterday and been reported missing by her boss. He described her as "very reliable." Parents deceased. The less-than-attractive photograph on her driver's license seemed to match, but it would have to be confirmed with fingerprints.

"If it's her, she just worked three doors down," Sanchez said. This area was referred to restaurant row for a reason. "She's a waitress. That's a little too close for comfort. I wonder if he saw it as a challenge or the location's just a coincidence."

"That's an interesting point. Why would he leave her so close to her place of work?"

"I don't know. Maybe he was hoping that someone who knew her would find her." Such cruelty depressed him.

After a hectic morning, he got confirmation that the autopsy would start at one thirty. He was sure Levant had got a call from the mayor's office and her boss, persuading her to hurry it along. Serial murders were always given top priority in the hopes of avoiding new victims.

At one fifteen, he made the familiar trek down to what they jokingly called Murder Central. Dr. Levant was pulling her gown and gloves on, intensity in her narrowed eyes. "I don't think this is going to be an easy one, is it, Detective?"

"Not many of them are."

"I wish there was a way to make the tests come back from the lab quicker. That would certainly help."

They moved over to the side of the waiting table and he sighed. "We'd have to have people in the lab working twenty-four hours a day to even start to cut down on the backlog. The bean counters will never let that happen."

"Sad, but true." She stepped up to the body as her assistant turned the recorder on. Elijah stood quietly as she recorded everyone's name and moved through the skin checks, teeth, and eyes, eventually helping her turn the body for a look at the back. "The body's almost pristine," she commented. "That's not much help."

When all was said and done, it was a repeat of Redding's procedure. They would have to wait for the blood tests. He stripped off his protective clothing, trying not to show his frustration, then thanked them and left. What the hell were they missing? This killer couldn't be that good, could he?

Chapter Seven

Christopher slipped through Dayle's apartment entrance with another couple, smiling his most personable smile and holding the door for them. God, people were morons, he thought as he rode up in the elevator with them. The come-hither smile the redhead sent his way didn't go unnoticed. *Not tonight, darling. I have more important things to accomplish than servicing you.*

By sheer luck, the security cameras on this floor were centered on the elevator. He simply pulled his collar up and turned his face away as he passed by them. Between his wide-brimmed hat and collar, they could prove nothing. Scanning the surrounding apartments twice as he looked for signs of activity, he confirmed no one paid any attention to him. He continued to stroll down the hall until the few people who lingered disappeared into other apartments.

Turning to face her door, he used the lock picks he'd practiced with to gain entrance to her unit in less than three minutes. The subtle click when the last tumbler gave way made his heart sing. The skills he'd learned in prison never failed to amaze him. He slipped inside the door, closing it behind him. Smiling, he tapped in the security code and the system light went green. Paying someone to hack in and get her code had only cost a thousand dollars—money well spent. That's what happened when the management company of your building kept a copy of your security code to allow maintenance access. *Sloppy, Dayle. So sloppy to allow such a thing.*

When would she ever learn that it was a waste of time to attempt to keep him out? It hadn't worked the last time. Why even try? She would never outsmart him.

Moving away from the entrance, he glanced around, taking note of the painstaking cleanliness everywhere. A burst of pride filtered through him. He'd taught her to be meticulous. When they'd been newlyweds, she'd been quite sloppy around the house, but that was nothing a few love taps couldn't cure. He'd broken her finger once, teaching her to scrub the floor. Now, everything gleamed from its own tidy place, the way it should. Prowling through the apartment, everything appeared organized to the last detail. The fact she had kept up her duties signaled she was more than ready for his triumphant return to her bed.

He searched through her spacious closet, inhaling the compelling citrus scent of her that lingered on her jackets. Her wardrobe consisted of too many boring suits, making him wince with displeasure. How could he make other men jealous if they couldn't glimpse her fabulous body and salivate? That would certainly have to change. The really slutty things were for his eyes only, but it was a woman's duty to taunt a man, giving him a promise of what's to come. She'd wear the damn pink lingerie he'd sent her whether she liked it or not.

There were no framed personal photographs of any kind clustered around the space, proving that this cop couldn't mean much to her. He searched further. When he opened the liquor cabinet, he felt annoyed that the labels weren't properly facing outward. He took a minute to fix the situation, chuckling to imagine how she'd react when she noticed. And she would notice, just as he intended she would.

When he entered her bedroom, he paused to enjoy the feminine accoutrements. She kept pretty, pastel-colored, glass perfume bottles on a tray which sat on her bureau. A piece of fine lace lay draped over the single chair. The arrangement said woman to him, and he breathed in her ambiance as if she were there with him. After some consideration, he decided to leave his latest, enthralling gift centered on her queen-size bed. He didn't bother with fancy wrapping this time, laying the four pieces on the comforter next to the pillow. Under the surface of every good girl was a naughty girl just waiting to break free. Ignoring the lure of her true desires was not the same as not possessing them. He was more than willing to help her explore them.

Just wait until she saw what he'd left, he thought gleefully as he let himself out of the apartment. *Just wait.*

****

Elijah took a much-needed break from his day to check in with Dayle. He rolled his shoulders and sat back in his chair, picking up his phone to text.

—*How's your day so far?*—

—*A case that's driving me mad. I can't wait for some peace and quiet*—

—*Go ahead and eat dinner whenever you feel like it. I'm going to be late*—

—*Okay. I'll grab some more clothes at the*

apartment first—

—Relax and enjoy. I'll see you later—

The Byzinski girl had been positively identified, but, just like last time, the autopsy hadn't provided any additional clues. They would have to wait on the blood tests and see if they provided any insight. She was an orphan, so there'd been no family to notify. Somehow that made the loss all the more tragic. The restaurant manager who'd called in the initial report, a big, hulking man, had cried like a baby when he'd been told of her fate. At least someone had cared about what happened to her. Sometimes, sadly, no one gave a damn.

He still sat neck deep in reports when his cellphone rang, the number showing it was Dayle on the other end. "Hi. Did you make it home okay?"

"N-no."

The shaky tone in her voice brought him to full alert in seconds. "What's wrong?"

"He's been in my apartment."

"Where are you?"

"I'm in the kitchen."

"Any signs that he's still there?"

"No."

"Okay, I'll be there in twenty minutes."

"Elijah—"

"I'll be right there, Dayle. Stay on the phone with me if you want."

He rushed down the stairs and out the door of the precinct. By the time he reached the garage, frightening scenarios battered him as he tried voicing the normal platitudes to keep her calm. On arrival, he didn't even wait for the elevator, vaulting up seven flights of stairs instead. As he hurried up the hall, gasping for breath, she opened the door. He didn't miss her expression of profound relief. Now that he could see her, a need for calm flooded him. He pulled her into his arms, holding her tight as her body trembled under his touch. "Are you okay?"

She sucked in a breath. "Just rattled. I'm sorry, I didn't mean to frighten you."

Not wanting to share her personal issues with nosy neighbors, they moved inside the apartment and shut the door. "Did he take anything?"

"Not that I can tell. He left something, though." Taking his hand, she led him into the bedroom and pointed at the four leather straps lying there.

He took a disbelieving look. "Bondage ties?"

She nodded and a flush stole up her cheeks. "He always wanted me to do that, but it didn't appeal to me."

"I'd say that from what you told me about him, it's a good thing you didn't take the chance. He doesn't seem to be capable of any form of restraint." He looked closer at the leather pieces and wondered if she'd seen the small, burned letters which spelled out, She Belongs to Me. He wondered if that was a message to him or were they sold that way? "Did you touch them?"

"No."

"Good." He pulled gloves from his pocket. "Get me a large, plastic closeable bag."

She scurried to the kitchen, digging through the pantry before returning with one. Grabbing the offending pieces, he slipped them inside and closed it. "You never know. We might get lucky and get a print." He doubted it, knowing all the criminal wisdom the man would have learned in prison. Setting the bag aside, he kissed her cheek. "I want you to pack enough clothes to keep you for a while. I don't want you coming back here by yourself until we solve this, even to pack."

"He's doing it all over again," she whispered and he saw tears well in the corners of her solemn eyes. "He's making me scared of my own shadow and putting you at risk, too."

Wrapping his arms around her, he kissed her forehead. "We'll put a stop to it, I promise. In the morning, I'll ask security to check the cameras and see if we caught sight of him. In the meantime, you'll be home with me. We both need food and some rest."

"But I interrupted your work. Don't you have to go back?"

"It's just research. I can do it just as easily from home."

She packed a bag in minutes while he changed the code on her alarm. They would try and figure out how he'd bypassed it later. He tucked a copy of the new code into her briefcase, so she could memorize it later. As he carried her luggage, she grabbed her briefcase along with a few suits. Despite the alarming reason for her call, it felt comforting to be going home together.

****

Christopher waited and watched, leaning against a wall across the street from Dayle's apartment building. As expected, the persistent Detective Black raced to her side mere moments after she'd arrived home. *How predictable, this unwelcome white knight.* Sure enough, shortly after he arrived, he whisked Dayle away, both of them laden with her things. All Christopher had to do was follow the other man's car from a short distance away, knowing he wouldn't get spotted in the linear rush of evening traffic.

It was hard to imagine what kind of pathetic dive this guy lived in as he wound through the congested city streets. Dayle certainly had to earn significantly more than this loser. She didn't belong in a damn hovel. Dating down was what she deserved to remind her what she'd lost when he got sentenced to jail.

After a short drive, they pulled out of traffic and parked in a nice neighborhood, on a street lined with older houses. Easing to a stop at the curb a few houses down, he stared, surprised by the tidy brownstone with its neatly maintained lawn. *How in hell could a cop afford that?* It was New York, after all, home of the over-priced everything.

Black locked the car, an obvious work ride, and lifted her suitcase out of the trunk. He led the way and Dayle followed him up the stairs, waiting as he unlocked. When he did, he stepped back to allow her to slip in front of him. Both disappeared inside, and the closing door blocked his view after that.

Christopher drove away after a few minutes of observation, determined not to attract unwanted attention from meddlesome neighborhood watchdogs. Under the convenient cover of night, he could return and investigate further. He thought it odd that Dayle felt comfortable enough to stay in this man's house after such a short acquaintance. Just how serious were they? She hadn't even slept with him for three months when they first met.

The unwelcome and telling comparison made his temper flare. He drove away, realizing he had to figure out some way to ensure he removed Black from the picture as soon as possible.

****

After removing their coats, Elijah and Dayle curled up on the sofa, enjoying a glass of wine in an effort to relax. "I think you need to notify your boss about your problems with your ex-husband, just so he's in the loop."

She sighed. "I know that I should, but I'd rather not. It's embarrassing. I hate feeding the gossip mill."

He rubbed a hand down her arm. "I understand that, but the more eyes we have keeping you safe, the better. What if he shows up at work?"

"Let me think about it. In the meantime, can we talk about something else?"

"Of course."

She'd tried to wait until he told her himself, but curiosity won out. "Where do you go on Friday mornings? I know it's none of my business, but I can't help wondering about it."

He took so long to respond, she thought he might be trying to avoid an answer, but then he spoke. "I go to the local cemetery and put a rose on a friend's grave."

Now, she felt like an idiot. "I'm sorry for being nosy. You've just been so open about everything else."

Leaning, he dropped a warm kiss on her cheek. "You can ask me anything. It's fine." After a pause, he spoke again. "Do you know who Cara Belton was?"

"Yes. She was the serial killer who killed all those abusive men." She felt him wince as she said it. "One of my co-workers filled me in when I first arrived. I know you were lead detective on that case."

"Sanchez and I were the lead investigators, yes."

She felt a sudden flare of guilt. "I should confess that I was searching for a stapler the other day and found a letter from her to you. I apologize for reading it. I hadn't meant to snoop. My curiosity gets the better of me sometimes."

Her admission made him feel a little uncomfortable for a moment, then he remembered the reason for her struggle with trust. Shuffling his legs, he turned to face her. "I don't want there to be any secrets between us, Dayle. Her case affected me in a way that changed my life. When I discovered exactly how horrific her childhood had been, I wished I could have been there when she was younger to save her. And for a long time, I just couldn't get that desire out of my head."

"She wasn't a helpless child, but you imagined her as one."

"Yes."

"What happened to change that?"

He smiled. "A couple of things, actually. Sanchez kicked my butt until I got back on my feet, for one. I love her for that. And then I realized the best way to pay tribute to Cara was to use her money to help as many women and children as I can. In a way, that changes her legacy to something positive."

"I'm surprised no one at work made a fuss about you inheriting that much money from a serial killer."

He shrugged. "Apparently, it's only a big deal if you receive a payout from a living person, because it might be considered a bribe for special treatment. I assured the commissioner that I would be using the entire inheritance for community projects and they were satisfied with that assurance."

"What was she like?"

He took a sip of wine before answering. "Brilliant, tortured, witty, and almost childlike at times. Her changing psyche was what made her so difficult to deal with throughout the case. In another life, with the blessing of a normal family like mine, she would have been an accomplished career woman."

"Such a waste," Dayle murmured. "Such a heartbreaking thing for a child to suffer." She met his gaze. "Do you mind if I go to her grave with you on Friday morning?"

"I'd like that." A while later, they retired to bed and slept.

The next day passed in a blur of paperwork and pounding the pavement, searching for clues to save the next victim. Other than stopping for a meal or two along the way, nothing out of the ordinary helped them along.

Friday morning offered a gorgeous, sunny day, one of those New York City days when the world seems reborn. They walked, hand in hand, to the graveyard fifteen minutes away. Elijah opened the wrought-iron gate for Dayle, shuddering at the shriek the hinges made. "I keep forgetting to bring a can of oil with me to remedy that."

They strolled down aisles of graying headstones, past the occasional bouquet of flowers or wreaths brought by loved ones. A breeze whispered through the trees that lined the gravel path. He gestured to a simple stone marker, the gentle carving around her name the only decoration. Beneath the dates, it said, "The nights are endless without you." She wondered about the emotional words and he explained. "It's from an old letter that I found once in a book. When she broke into my house, she found it and thought it had personal significance. It's rather poetic, though, and I just thought her marker should have something besides her name."

The story brought tears to her eyes. "You are an incredibly kind man, and you have a romantic heart."

Embarrassment colored his cheeks, and he squeezed her hand. He lay the rose he'd clipped from his mother's rose bush on the grass in front of the stone. He cleared his throat. "Don't tell anyone. I have to keep up appearances, you know."

She smiled up at him, brushing her fingers against his lapel. "It's our little secret." His actions touched something in her heart she'd thought was long dead. He thought to remember Cara with kindness while others were quick to forget.

A few minutes passed in silence. He glanced at his watch. "We'd better go or we'll be late." They went back a slightly different way, ducking into the bakery to grab croissants they could eat in the car. Work beckoned.

****

Elijah dropped her off at her office, watching carefully until she was safely inside the revolving glass doors. As soon as he arrived at the precinct, he received a brief text requesting his presence in his lieutenant's office. His boss stood as he entered and offered him a coffee. "Just finished one, thanks."

"Have a seat." They both sat and got comfortable. The other man glanced out the window. "I've been meaning to talk to you about something when our case load quiets down, but it never does, does it?"

"No, sir. I'm afraid not."

He steepled his fingers, meeting Elijah's gaze. "I'm not sure if you've heard any rumors, but I'm planning to retire in nine months."

He'd overheard quiet discussions behind closed doors but told no one. "I'm sorry to hear that, sir. I've been very satisfied under your command and appreciate everything you've taught me."

"Thank you. As you probably know, an outgoing leader is quite often asked who he would recommend for the position. When the time comes, I would like you to consider becoming my replacement."

The comment surprised and pleased him. "I'm flattered. There are others here, though, who have been on the job longer than I have. This would be an accelerated promotion for me."

"We have some excellent detectives here, that's true, but not everyone is leadership material. You've had several difficult major cases in a row, and your swift handling of them caught everyone's attention. Both the commissioner and the mayor have been quite impressed by the way you handled your inheritance from Ms. Belton. Committing all of the money to local charities showed them your character. They were very impressed." He waited for a response. After Elijah thanked him, he continued. "Besides yourself, who would you say is the strongest homicide detective here?"

"Sanchez."

He smiled. "You didn't hesitate. Why is she the strongest?"

"She's thorough with details and has terrific computer skills. Her ability dealing with witnesses is unparalleled. And she's an excellent shot which never hurts."

"What's her greatest weakness?"

He had to be honest. "The political end of things. I believe she would tell you that herself if asked."

Smiling, he said, "So, she's a wonderful detective, but she couldn't do administration."

"It's true that I don't think she'd be interested in that particular role, yes, sir."

He narrowed his gaze. "And who, currently, is our weakest detective?"

"Hadley."

"You didn't hesitate there either."

"No, sir."

"Tell me why."

"Unfortunately, he's more interested in his own advancement than he is doing an excellent job. He complains constantly. A lot of important details slip by him. Frankly, if Davis wasn't so easygoing, he would have asked for a new partner a long time ago."

"And if you were in my shoes, what would you do with him?"

"I'd try to interest him in another, less demanding, department where he might be better suited to the work."

He smiled. "Given your opinion, you might be glad to hear that's exactly what I'm doing at this moment. Robbery needs another detective, and I'll try to persuade him that he could advance more quickly there." Now, he leaned back and relaxed. "Assessing staff can be an important part of my job, and you come by it naturally. I think your calm and thoughtful disposition is invaluable in our kind of work. That said, do you think you would be content no longer working cases directly?"

"I think so, sir. It's a different skill set, of course, but equally important. I'm younger than most for this type of position, though. Do you think I would have the necessary support from the powers above?"

He nodded. "We've talked about your advancement in theory. It's safe to say that you would likely have their support, barring any unexpected developments." Taking a sip of his coffee, he continued. "If you're interested, I'll start including you in some meetings that would get your feet wet, so to speak. For now, give it some thought, won't you?"

"I will, sir. Thank you for the vote of confidence." Reading the other man's body language that their talk had ended, he stood.

"And give Dayle my best."

"I will."

****

The killer sat back on his favorite old sofa with a full glass of malbec wine. He twirled the blood-colored liquid with a happy sigh. Delivering Katy to her maker had been a remarkable high, comprising his best scene yet. Locating her young body to be discovered by such a public venue was another stroke of genius. Theater and the public should work hand in hand, one offering a different type of splendid performance and one a grateful audience.

She'd been so excited about the rare opportunity she'd been offered, her pale cheeks flushed with excitement. The young woman had attained celebrity, after all. Her art combined with his would be celebrated on the front pages for days to come. The brilliant young actress had trusted him to deliver her ultimate fate and so he had. True, she wouldn't receive the promised paycheck, but she'd been gifted with a much more incredible opportunity. A place in history belonged to her. Her story was one for the ages, due to be revered by thousands as time progressed.

Some of the plebian wannabes in this theater community didn't understand his unlimited potential, but he had proven them wrong once again. Their jeering insults belonged in the past. Brilliance is often overlooked by even the most discerning observer, but not anymore. Instead, now his work soared to public acclaim which, surely, was long overdue. He so richly deserved an award, but he would have to settle for the pleasure of his staggering accomplishment. After all, ultimate perfection is its own reward.

Chapter Eight

Sanchez filled both of their coffee mugs and dropped Elijah's off at his desk with a smirk. The welcome aroma swirled between them. "So, are you and Stockard shackin' up for the long haul, or is buying a snazzy ring in your future?"

He narrowed his eyes and frowned at her. "Why, are you spreading marital bliss around now that you've taken a leap?"

"Sure, why not? Misery loves company and all that crap."

He leaned back to meet her gaze. "There are extenuating circumstances right now." Telling her about the latest developments with Dayle's ex-husband took a few minutes.

His partner's response was typical. "The world is full of assholes," she declared, throwing her arms wide. "So, what do we have to do to stop this one?"

He appreciated that she didn't just blow it off as none of her concern. "I don't know. I'm trying to figure out how to best protect her when she doesn't want anyone to know about him."

"She didn't report it?"

"No, but she's got a point. He hasn't been caught doing anything illegal yet."

"Breaking and entering."

"I can't prove it was him. The security film just showed a guy in a hat and coat. Not even a sliver of skin. And we still don't know where he got her security code."

She frowned. "Be sure to tell her if you're not around, me and Ray will help her out."

Smiling, he tapped her shoulder. "I appreciate that." He knew he could always count on them. They were his family now.

"She should be safe enough at work, and we can take turns escorting her back and forth if you want."

"Thanks. That's what we might have to do until I figure out a plan of action. If I can get her to agree to it, that is. She finds it all pretty embarrassing." Time for him to put that worry away for now. "What have you got to do this morning?"

"We collected security tapes from the three nearby restaurants. Why don't I run through them and see if I can find anything interesting? And I'm still working on tracking down the emails from Svengali to Redding."

"Sounds good." Elijah sat at his desk, wondering what clue they were missing. These two crimes had an almost theatrical flair. There appeared to be some kind of sentiment attached to them as well. No bruising, no signs of aggression, almost as if they had feelings for them. No signs they had fought back. Had they known each other? But, so far, they hadn't uncovered any personal connection between them.

He left for a few moments to freshen up in the bathroom and stretch his legs. It was amazing what a splash of cold water on your face could do to get you re-energized. When he re-entered the office, he found Sanchez hunched over the computer muttering, "There you are, you bastard." A note of satisfaction colored her tone.

"You find something?"

She waved him over, impatience creating a frown on her face. "Look at this freak." Winding the recording back, she moved so he could lean over her shoulder. He watched the grainy image, recognizing the back alley where they found the victim. After a few seconds, a person in a long black cape swirled into the frame, carrying the girl in his arms. An over-sized hood totally obscured his face. He placed her against the dumpster with a gentle motion, pausing to arrange her wig with one gloved hand. Straightening, he peered at her as if to double-check his work, then backed out of the frame, one cautious step at a time.

"Damn it. We can't see a thing," she said. "He knew the freakin' camera was there. The recording's a waste of time."

"Not necessarily. We can hazard a good guess at his height by comparing it to the height of the dumpster. That type is about five and a half feet to the lid. When he straightened, he stood about four inches taller."

"So, between five-nine and five-ten?"

"Yes. Let's doublecheck." They watched it over and over, but decided their guess was accurate. They hoped for a visual that would lead them to a vehicle, but none of the cars moved around that time. "He must have parked in an area the cameras didn't reach. So, he clearly did his homework."

They eventually turned the recording off, rubbing their eyes. He considered the film they'd just watched. "Does it occur to you that both of these crimes have kind of a vintage feel to them?"

"What do you mean?"

"The two stories are from old books, one from 1837 and the other the 17th century. The cape from the first crime reminds me of old-time mysteries. And now he's using a cape as well. Is it possible our killer is older than the average man who does this kind of thing?"

"Please don't tell me you know the date of those books just from memory."

He shook his head, smiling. "Children's books are hardly my specialty. I looked them up."

"Oh, thank God. Cause it'd be kinda creepy if you knew a lot about children's books."

"I guess it would be." He took a moment to consider the possibilities. "Let's find out if either victim had an interest in literature or theater. Seems to me the first victim had high school trophies for acting in her bedroom."

Her fingers zoomed across the keyboard and information on the screen passed in a blur. "Bingo. Both victims took theater classes in high school. Different schools, though, and different teachers."

"Okay. It's getting too late today, but tomorrow, we need to pay a visit to both teachers. Let's find out how interested these girls were in that class and who that put them in contact with."

"Sounds like a plan."

They left the precinct at eight thirty, Ray picking up his partner while Elijah headed to pick up Dayle at her office. When they arrived home, he smiled. "I have a surprise for you." He opened the door and she heard an ominous beeping. She rocked back a step. "It's okay.

I had a security system put in first thing this morning." Punching in some numbers, he waved her inside, locking the door behind them.

Touched, she looked up at him. "You did that just for me?"

He dropped a chaste kiss on her cheek. "I have a friend who owns a security company. I thought you might feel more at ease having one to turn on if I'm not here."

Wrapping her arms around his waist, she tucked her head into his shoulder. "That is so thoughtful of you."

"Hey," he whispered, "You're my girl, right? There's not much I wouldn't do for you."

They made an easy dinner with pasta and vegetables. Afterwards, they curled on the couch and he told her about his conversation with Lieutenant Porter.

"Elijah, that's amazing! Were you surprised or did you know something was in the works?"

"No, I really wasn't expecting anything of the kind. Porter really has been an amazing boss. When he first put me on all the media stuff, I was shocked. You know most departments have one person to handle all that."

"That's true."

"Anyway, I realize now that he was trying to raise my profile in the department with this in mind. So, I'm glad I didn't get too cranky about it."

"That's smart of him. Like it or not, media plays a huge part now in our lives. There are eyes everywhere. How soon will he be retiring?"

"Not for nine months."

"Do you think your other superiors will support you?"

"He seems to think they will and that's good enough for me. I'm not telling anybody but you and Sanchez though. If it comes about, not everyone will be thrilled about it."

"That's the same everywhere. If you can keep eighty percent of the people happy, that's about as good as it gets."

"True."

"Have you told Sanchez yet?"

"No. I wanted to tell you first."

"How's she going to react?"

He grinned. "I'll have some verbal abuse headed my way. It'll be in Spanish, though, so I won't understand most of it anyway."

"She's going to hate getting another partner."

"That's true, but I have what I think is a rather clever plan."

"I knew you probably would. What is it?"

"If his boss lets me, I'm going to pull Seth to assist in as many murder cases as possible so he'll get some valuable experience. Hopefully, then, I can make a case for him to move from his starting division to homicide a little faster than planned."

"That's sneaky. If you get the promotion, you're hoping to partner him with Sanchez, aren't you?"

"Yes. They'd be a great match. He's patient, and she can show him the ropes. And he actually likes women as I do and won't feel threatened by her."

She cocked her head. "He's one of the few people you'd trust her with, isn't he?"

"Yes." He took her hand and kissed the back of it. "It's a little scary when things work out so well for everyone, isn't it?"

"Yes." At her laughing reply, they snuggled in to watch some television.

****

Back at his apartment, Christopher reared his arm back and smashed a crystal glass against the wall, relishing the sound of destruction. Kicking at the resulting shards, he cursed. He'd been preparing to enter Black's house through the back door when the security men had showed up to install an extensive alarm system. If only he'd entered the night before as he'd originally planned, but his plans had been thwarted by a noisy neighbor who had shown up, walking a damn dog, and asked if he was lost. He had pretended to be, saying he'd misread the correct address by one digit. Even then, the persistent man had watched until he disappeared around the corner. *Interfering bastard.*

Timing meant everything, and now he'd been screwed by an unforeseen circumstance. He had planned to destroy the contents of the man's house and leave a threatening letter for Dayle. She needed to know this affair put not just her, but her lover, at risk. Lacking technical skills meant he didn't have a clue how to bypass the security. He'd lucked out at Dayle's place. In this case, though, he'd looked up the company the detective had used and learned their systems were the best in the city. Wishing he had one of his former cellmates to advise him wasted valuable time.

Damn it! Now, he had to come up with a whole new plan of attack. Remembering the way Dayle had cowered at his feet that final night of their marriage motivated him. That experience was better than any cocaine he'd ever snorted, giving him a high that eclipsed any other. The fear on her face had turned him on more than any single thing in his thrilling life.

He wanted to relive it. He wanted her to grovel and beg for his favor.

And, this time, his knife wouldn't just scar her. If she didn't bow to him after he used her in every degrading way possible and terrorized her lover, he'd finish her. He'd make damn sure she'd never have a life without him.

****

Dr. Levant was on the phone earlier than expected for a Saturday. When he saw it was her name on the screen, he rushed to answer. "Good morning, Doc. You're up bright and early. I hope that means you have some good news for me."

"It's news, Detective, although a little more puzzling than helpful under the circumstances. I couldn't sleep, because this case is driving me nuts. Well, more nuts than usual."

He sighed. "Well, that's how this case has been so far. What have you got?"

"It's the Redding girl's blood results. The GHB count is off the charts. The question is, why use a date rape drug and then not assault her?"

Of all the things, he'd expected, that wasn't even on the list. "No sign of poison?"

"No. We're missing something. Healthy twenty-something-year-old girls don't die for no clear reason."

"No, they don't. Damn it. So, how do we proceed?"

"I'm going to have another look at her this afternoon to make sure I didn't miss something. I also just ordered a wider screen to include all the more rare possibilities and put a rush on it."

"Okay. Let me know if you find anything. I appreciate the extra effort."

"You'll know as soon as I do." The fact that she hung up without saying goodbye was a sign of her frustration. When he passed the news onto Sanchez, she took a moment to consider the news, her upper lip tugged between her teeth.

"Maybe he just wanted her to be easier to control. That's what those drugs do, right? They make you easier to manipulate."

He should have known that. This case was draining his intellect. "You're right. So, if the drugs were stage one, so what the hell was stage two?"

"That's Levant's job. She'll figure it out." They filled the hours with work, waiting for a breakthrough that would kick this case into high gear.

Chapter Nine

Dayle smiled when she saw Sanchez enter the restaurant. As she looked her way, she waved and the detective headed over. "How ya doin?"

"Great. How's the baby?"

She lowered herself to the bench, rubbing her stomach. "The little stinker's starvin' all the time, so I know it's my kid."

"It was nice of you to ask me to lunch. I usually stay chained to my desk, but I really should get out more often." She'd been curious about the sudden invitation, but pleased nonetheless. It was a rare chance to talk to Elijah's partner without a crowd around.

Sanchez shrugged. "Well, I know you and Elijah are getting kinda serious. I guess I thought maybe we should get used to hangin' out together."

"I agree." They paused to discuss the menu choices. Dayle picked a salad, and Sanchez groaned.

"I guess I should do that, too." She didn't look very happy about the prospect.

"Why don't you get a burger with a side of salad? That way, both you and the baby are happy."

Sanchez grinned. "I like your style." Waiting until after the waitress took the order, she met Dayle's gaze. "Can I just get something out of the way?"

Unsure what kind of comment might be coming,

she answered, "Sure."

"You're not just screwin' around with Elijah, are you? I mean, I'm a bigtime fan of great sex, but he needs more than that. He needs the whole enchilada and all that shit. He deserves it more than anyone I know."

It touched her, this feisty little firebrand looking out for her friend and partner. She met her gaze, smiling. "I think it's wonderful the way you look out for him and vice versa. And, just between you and me, I'm crazy about him. I'm happier with him than I've ever been with anyone." She would keep any talk of love between her and Elijah for now.

The worry lines in Sanchez's face relaxed. "Jeez, that's great. It's just that he's had lousy luck with women, and he's such a great guy. I saw the way he looks at you from the very beginning, and I don't want him to get hurt."

"Well, I'm very hopeful about the future. Does that make you more comfortable?"

"That's good enough for me." She rapped her knuckles on the table. "Elijah told me about the problems with your ex-husband."

They'd moved from the best of times to the worst in one simple sentence. The muscles in her stomach clenched, and she tried to relax. "I feel like such a whiner, but I'm really at a loss about how to deal with him."

Sanchez's jaw tightened. "Oh, we got ways of dealing with scum like him. We just have to catch him in the act."

"Easier said than done. He's managed to work his out-of-control behavior into a fine art, I'm afraid."

"He'll make a mistake. They always do. You know

how to shoot?"

"Yes."

"Got a concealed carry license?"

"Yes."

"Start carrying every day until we catch him. If you haven't practiced in a while, we can take you to the range and work on it together. You gotta go to war on this guy, you know what I mean?"

She nodded. "I think that's an excellent idea." She didn't mention that she'd have to buy a gun. She could do that. The waitress brought their food, and they talked as they ate about her plans for the baby.

After they were finished eating, Sanchez lifted her napkin and wiped her mouth. "You're really slim. Do you ever eat a burger?"

"Sometimes."

"One of those fake ones they claim tastes like real meat?"

She laughed. "Oh, no, even I don't like them. They're terrible."

"See? We got stuff in common after all. I like real cow."

She laughed, then sobered. "Can I ask you a strange question?"

The word strange caused curiosity in the other woman's face. "Sure, I guess. I guess it depends on what you consider strange."

Flushing, she reassured her. "Nothing too weird. Elijah told me about putting a rose on Cara Belton's grave when I asked about it. I guess I just wondered what your take was on that whole situation. Her death touched him, but, in your opinion, was it something more?"

Sanchez looked relieved as if she'd expected something more dire. "It's true that he had a difficult time comin' back after that one. I had a hard time understanding it myself, to be honest." Sitting back, she rubbed her belly. "In our business, there are certain crimes that hit you harder than others. For Elijah, it happened to be this particular case. I think he just felt helpless at the end. He really wanted to save her, and he felt like he failed."

"Did you ever feel like she could be saved?"

She shook her head, her eyes somber. "Nah. When you take lives for so many years, even bastards that deserve it, I think it warps your soul. Elijah wanted to save her, but he couldn't recognize that he was years too late." She took a drink. "They did have a weird connection, though. I think it's because she recognized him as a good man, and she'd never experienced one before. All she'd known were deviants."

"What a horrible life." She met Sanchez's gaze. "Thank you for helping him through it."

Embarrassment had her twitching. "I didn't do anything any friend wouldn't have done."

"Well, you know he keeps to himself a lot. You and Ray are really his only close friends besides me."

"Pretty sure he's way past friendly with you." She grinned. "Seth and Pamela are part of the in crowd now, too. We'll make a party animal out of your man yet. And who would have guessed some damn ex-beauty queen would fit in with a bunch of cops and lawyers."

"Oh, I didn't know Pamela was a beauty queen, but it doesn't shock me. Life can be surprising, can't it?"

She snorted a laugh. "Hell, yeah. If you'd have told me I'd ever be married, I woulda laughed my ass off, never mind getting pregnant, too." She glanced at her watch. "Damn it. I'd better run." Pulling out some bills, she dropped them on the table. "Listen, if Elijah ain't around and you need help with your asshole ex, call. Don't hesitate. Me and Ray are always a few minutes away. We'll come runnin'."

She felt a surge of emotion at her simple offer of protection. "Thanks. I'll remember that."

"Later, tater." Sanchez hustled through the crowd, stepped out the door and disappeared into the passing pedestrians. Dayle sipped on her drink as the waitress removed the dishes, thankful for the friends she was making here. It had been years since she'd had a simple meal with a girlfriend which was a pathetic state of affairs. Gathering up her purse and jacket, she made for the door and headed back to work.

****

Elijah insisted they all take the day off on Sunday. They had been working long, hard hours. Both baby and momma needed a rest. He knew if he didn't take one, too, she'd never agree, so he spent the day with Dayle and refused to feel guilty about it.

Finally, on Monday, they took a welcome step forward with the case. The awaited call came after they'd all grabbed lunch. Dr. Levant called, sounding both guilty and relieved. Elijah put her on speaker so Sanchez could hear. "On re-examination, I found a miniscule injection site way down in between her big toe and the next. He must have used a very small needle. We could barely see it, even with our best magnifying glass."

"Sneaky bastard," Sanchez said.

"Exactly. Once I found it, we checked Byzinski

and she has it too, in exactly the same place, right next to the big toe."

Elijah tried to imagine the killer's moves. "So, he gives them a drink with the GHB and then when they're relaxed, he gets them to lie down and doses them."

"Yes. Now, all we have to do is find out exactly what he doses them with. I called in a favor and they're rushing the results on the advanced screen, so cross your fingers. This might be our big break. If it's something weird, it's easier to track."

He felt some relief. "Thanks, Doc. We'll be waiting for your call."

Chapter Ten

The next morning dawned a little too early for anyone's liking. The long hours were taking their toll. Instead of working on a divide and conquer format, Elijah wanted Sanchez beside him during their school visits. Two sets of eyes and ears could be helpful. They edged their way through the last of the morning rush hour traffic. The first school they visited was St. Andrews, crammed on three city blocks downtown. Parking in a crowded lot, they made their way inside. They ducked around groups of kids milling the halls and located the front office. At the reception desk, they introduced themselves to the seated woman inside and asked where they could find Thomas Hatcher, the theater teacher who'd taught Cathy Redding. The plump, gray-haired receptionist gave a wide smile. "He should be in his office at this time of day. Let me check."

Elijah smiled. "If you can just tell me his room number, we can find our way."

"I'd like to do that, but we have to check in with the principal first. It's protocol."

She stood and led the way to the door. The principal, an older woman with a stern visage, had the unfortunate name of Ms. Peony Meanie. Her expression was enough to make him fear detention for the first time in his life. They explained the situation to her and she said nothing except, "Okay, you have my permission to proceed." He wondered for a moment if she'd been in the army, judging by her attitude and her painfully correct posture. After getting her permission, she escorted them out of the office and watched their progress down the hall with suspicion.

With the room number provided, they walked down the long corridor, ignoring the curious glances of a few remaining students who weren't already in class. Long lines of battle-scarred metal lockers lined the halls, some creative suggestions scrawled in red marker on the doors. The fluorescent lights above exposed the expected wear and tear from years of students. Murmurs from the various classrooms could be heard. According to the rectangular plate by the entrance, the last room on the left belonged to Hatcher. They stopped to knock on the heavy oak door. "Come in," a deep masculine voice responded.

Elijah swung the door open, allowing Sanchez to precede him. A man approximately Elijah's age stood to greet them, smiling. His thick chestnut hair swept off his face in a deliberate, sculpted wave. His ocean blue eyes sparkled. "Hello," he said stretching his arm over the desk to shake hands with firm confidence. "I'm Thomas Hatcher. How can I help you?"

Elijah introduced themselves, and their identification made the skin on his forehead wrinkle. "When the front office called to say you were on the way, I must say my curiosity was piqued. We're not in any trouble, I hope."

"Not at all." They took seats in the makeshift wooden chairs, and the teacher followed their example.

"Your principal indicated that you might be able to help us. We have a few questions about a former student."

"What division are you folks from?"

"Homicide."

Shock stole his smile. "Oh, no. A former student is dead?"

"I'm afraid so. Do you remember Cathy Redding?"

His face paled. "Of course. She was an excellent student. Are you saying she was murdered?"

"Yes. She was found in a local park last Saturday night."

"Good God." He snapped his fingers. "Oh, my goodness. I saw the headline about a woman's murder, but I didn't notice her name. What happened?"

"I'm afraid we are in the beginning stages of the inquiry. You say she was an excellent student. What kinds of roles did she take on in your class?"

"We perform a lot of plays here during the course of the year. I believe they don't learn much about theater unless they actually take an active part."

"I see. That makes sense. Was Cathy really interested or was she just here to fulfill her grade requirements?"

"Oh, she loved it. She frequently got a major part in our shows. She really enjoyed getting immersed in her characters. Took it more seriously than most of her classmates."

Elijah mentioned the two children's stories and asked if they'd ever used them on stage here at the school.

"Oh, no. That's a little childish for my taste. We tend to employ the works of Shakespeare and other classics. If we feel daring, maybe the works of a few modern playwrights."

"As far as you can remember, was there ever a part which required her to wear a red velvet cape?"

"Nothing that springs to mind, but I try to keep a file of details on our plays. Let me see if I can find my notes from those years." He turned to his computer and they waited as he searched, his fingers flying over the keys. After a few minutes' delay, he said, "No, I'm not seeing anything that would include a cape of any kind. I'm sorry. What does that have to do with her passing?"

Ignoring the question he couldn't answer, Elijah continued. "Did she ever have any problems with any boys or male staff here at school that you know of?"

He gave a little groan. "Oh, I could tell you more than you'd ever want to know about teenagers. They love their daily dramas. But Cathy was quite level-headed, despite her dream of being on stage. And she wasn't much one for chasing boys although they certainly chased her. Of all my students, I would have said she was the least likely one to get in trouble." He paused, frowning. "As far as staff are concerned, well, we keep an eye out for that kind of thing. To my knowledge, there's never been any issues."

"Thank you for being so helpful." He passed him a business card. "If you can think of anything else that might be of any assistance, please give us a call. And I'd appreciate it if you could keep the details of our questions to yourself."

"Of course." He walked them to the door and closed it again as they walked away.

They got caught right after a bell rang, and it took a few minutes to wade through the crowd of students changing classes and lolling around. A few students stopped to stare, well aware he and Sanchez didn't belong. Finally, they broke free and exited. Back in the car, he asked Sanchez for her impressions. "Hatcher's kind of a pretty boy, but it's hard not to like him. I bet you most of his students are female."

"I agree. It feels like this might actually result in a lead though. I think these crimes have something to do with their love of theater."

"Well, I'd bet good money on your instincts any day, so, based on previous experience, let's keep on it." She pulled both an orange and a chocolate bar out of her purse and ate them on the way to the next school. He declined a piece of both.

Our Lady of Xavier was on a different spectrum than the previous school. Elegant wrought-iron fences surrounded the entire property, and a security guard manned the gate. He told them where to park, and Elijah noticed him pick up the phone, probably to notify someone, as they drove away.

Consequently, an older woman in a pristine gray suit greeted them at the top of the front steps. She offered a professional smile, clearly conjured from long experience. "Good morning, detectives. My name is Beatrice Fallwood. I'm the vice-principal here. How may I help you?"

They explained the unfortunate reason for their visit. Her smile dissipated into a frown. "I'm afraid I heard about Katy on the news last night. A terrible business." That was likely why she'd been ready and waiting. She lifted a hand to gesture them inside. "If you follow me to my office, I'll see if I can locate Mr. Pemberton. He's in charge of our theater program."

Doing as she requested would keep everyone calm,

so they followed protocol. A brief call informed them that the teacher they wanted to interview was with a class on stage and she accompanied them to the entrance of the small theater. "I wish you luck," she said, excusing herself, and he wondered how she meant it.

It didn't take long to figure out. They entered and started down the long, sloping steps to the stage. As they approached, a man whirled to face them, his expression far from contented. "I told the staff absolutely no interruptions! Why are you here?"

He made it sound as if he had a more elevated position than mere staff. Elijah noticed that the students on the stage cowered under his glare. Elias Pemberton wore an extravagant white chemise more at home on a painter. Black pants underneath flowed, giving him a rather feminine appearance.

He and Sanchez pulled their badges and, this time, she spoke first. "Detectives Black and Sanchez, homicide. We won't take much of your time. We just have a few questions about a former student."

"The past is nothing while the present is an ongoing battle." He clearly intended his dramatic words to impress, but his attempt failed miserably.

She raised her eyebrows, and Elijah shook his head, not knowing the origin of the quote. Soldiering on, she said, "Do you remember Katy Byzinski?"

The kids on the stage creept closer, and he waved his flapping arms at them in a shooing motion. "Take a ten-minute break." After the students left, he turned back to them. "Yes, I remember Katy. She was another stunningly average actor in an ocean of them."

"She was murdered on Wednesday."

His face showed no change of expression. He simply looked more annoyed. "Yes, I know. I'm quite capable of reading the newspaper." He tapped his foot. "So?"

You'd have to search a long time to find empathy in this man. He managed to keep his dislike to himself. "Did she have any parts in your plays while she was here?"

"Yes, of course. They are all required to participate unless they work as stage crew instead. We save those slots for those who are smart but untalented as actors."

"Was she talented?"

"Not at all, but you still have to let them take part. Otherwise, the pathetic creatures who gave birth to them will complain bitterly to anyone stupid enough to listen to their constant whining."

She mentioned the children's books. "Have you ever used them in performances here?"

"No, no, what a ghastly idea." Melodrama poured from every feature of his face. "You might perform such stories in grade school, but that's it. I have a higher calling."

They asked about any shows that involved a cape. "How incredibly plebian," he responded. "That might be suitable for a magician's act, but I would hope I would never resign myself to such a mediocre interpretation of wardrobe."

Elijah knew this line of questioning would be useless, but he had to try. "Did she have any problems with anyone while in your class? Especially male students or staff?"

He lifted his nose as if smelling something foul. "I don't know, and I don't care. Their social squabbles matter little to me."

Elijah met Sanchez's gaze and saw agreement in her expression that they were wasting their precious time with this sanctimonious asshole. "Thank you for your time." Handing him a business card, he said, "If you should think of anything helpful, please give us a call." As they walked away, they saw him fire the card into a wasting garbage basket as if he hoped to score points.

They made their way down the long hall and out onto the steps. "What an asswipe," Sanchez said. "Why on earth do they keep an idiot like that on staff?"

"Let's consider the possibilities," Elijah replied. "He's probably connected somehow or his family donated to the school."

"That's pretty cynical for you."

"Want to place a wager on it?"

"Nah. I like my money too much."

Reaching the car, they slid inside. "Let's take a side trip," Elijah suggested. "The guy who owns the theater store where I got the information about the cape might be able to tell us something about these two teachers. His name's Victor Mann, and apparently, he's been around the business for years."

Winding through the traffic didn't take them very long for a change, and they lucked into a nearby parking space. On arrival, the store had a few customers and they waited for them to be served, wandering around the racks to entertain themselves. Discovering everything from knights' costumes to vampires' entertained them for a few minutes. Victor had nodded when they entered so he knew they were waiting. After about ten minutes, the other people cleared out, and he waved them over. "You're back and you brought a lovely lady with you." His eyes twinkled as he clasped her hand.

Sanchez snorted a chuckle. "I'm not a lady, I'm a cop."

Her reply didn't faze him. "Surely, you can be both. How may I be of service?"

"Do you have any dealings with the local high school theater teachers?"

"Certainly. We often loan them outfits for performances in exchange for advertising in their program. Good to support the local communities, you know."

"Have you had any dealings with Thomas Hatcher and Elias Pemberton?"

He smiled at the first name and winced at the second. Nodding, he said, "Talk about polar opposites. Hatcher is a rather charming young man who seems to actually enjoy the kids in his care. Pemberton, on the other hand, is a gasbag wannabe."

"That mirrors our initial impression."

Victor shook his head and gave a muted moan. "I honestly don't know how that horrible man gets away with it. He had one off Broadway role years ago and rides on those worn-out coattails to this day. No serious theater person will even stop to chat with him in case his renowned arrogance is contagious."

"Any helpful gossip you could share about either one? It won't go any further."

He pursed his lips and shoved his hair back out of his eyes. "There is some speculation that Hatcher might occasionally pay a little too much attention to the young women in his care. I've never seen anything to back that up, though. On the other side of the coin, if I remember correctly, Pemberton has been cautioned twice over his temper."

"Can you tell me the details?" Elijah asked as he made notes in his pad.

"Once was with a student. I believe he raised his hand in anger, and someone intervened before he slapped the mouthy child. The second time involved another teacher who had won an award he felt he deserved. That whole debacle was shoved under the rug, so to speak. The talk was that his family paid off the other man after he shoved him during a rather heated discussion."

"He comes from money?"

He smiled. "Oh, yes. His uncle is one of the school's major benefactors."

"That explains a lot."

Laughing, he said, "It does, doesn't it? Now, was that gossip at all helpful?"

"It was, actually. We appreciate it."

"Any luck with your case?"

"Baby steps, Victor. But every one helps." He tucked his pad away in his pocket. "Let me know if you think of anything else that might help."

"I certainly will."

At the last minute before leaving, he turned back towards the other man. "Have you ever seen the local production of old children's books done in play form?"

He tapped a finger on his chin, humming in thought. "Not that I can remember. I can ask around if it would help."

"I'd appreciate it. Let me know if anything comes from your enquiry."

"I'll do that."

They exited onto the busy street, ducking other pedestrians. As they walked to their car, Sanchez said, "He's quite a character."

"Yes, he is, but very inclined to help which is a nice change of pace. Can you do a deep dive on both of these men? I feel like the theater connection is what's going to break this case."

"Yup. What else?"

He sighed. "I have a press meeting at two. I'll just chase down the small stuff until then."

At one forty-five, he headed down to the crowded press room with the commissioner. As the clock ticked down to show time, he saw Pamela Clayton at the front and gave her a nod as he waited for his turn to speak. She seemed much happier since she started dating Seth. Her bombshell appearance had been toned down a bit, probably in response to Seth's preference for a natural look, but her smile told him all he needed to know.

When it came to be Elijah's turn to speak, he gave her the nod to ask the first question. "Are the Redding and Byzinski cases connected to the same killer?"

"That appears to be the case, but we are still in the early stages of investigation."

A young hotshot new to the game almost bowled a woman over to get his attention. Elijah gave him a break to let him speak. "Do you have any suspects?"

He and his boss had discussed how to deal with that question. "We have several people of interest who we are investigating further."

And a few more questions:

"Is it true that the victims were given a date rape drug?"

Damn it. Where did they hear that? "No comment, other than to make it clear that these victims were not sexually assaulted."

"Is Detective Sanchez also on the case?"

"Yes. She's hard at work behind the scenes as we speak."

"Do you think there are more murders coming from this killer?" He felt like saying yes, probably, but settled for "No comment." After a few more questions, he ended the session. Walking back to the office, he heard his name and turned. Pamela jogged to catch up. Her cameraman was nowhere in sight. "How are you?" She kept pace beside him.

"Great. How are you?"

She grinned. "Wonderful. I wanted a chance to thank you."

"For what?"

"For introducing me to Seth."

"You're welcome. Can I assume things are going well, then?"

She nodded. "He's honestly the nicest man I've met in years. He's kind and thoughtful, not to mention really attractive. A veritable prince among the toads in this particular pond."

"I know he's pretty happy to spend time with you, too."

"I hope so. How's Dayle?"

"Good. She has a lot on her plate right now, but maybe when things calm down, the four of us should have dinner."

"We would love that." She glanced at her watch as they approached the precinct. "I'd better run. Stay safe."

He noticed she'd started saying those last two words after she was attacked a few months ago. Sanchez had saved her, but been knifed herself for intervening. Was it a sign of their convoluted lives that all he had to worry about now was his girlfriend's ex-husband and a killer in love with children's books? That along with keeping Sanchez and her brewing baby safe.

Well, at least they were never bored.

Chapter Eleven

Elijah found Sanchez resting her head on her desk. "You okay?" He looked down at her, concerned.

"Yeah." She lifted her head, yawning. "How depressing is that? I need a little nap in the afternoons now. Might as well be a grandma."

"You have to take care of my niece or nephew, right?" He rubbed her back, a perk she asked for now and then. "You need to go home early?"

"Jeez, I'm not eighty, I'm pregnant."

Her response made him grin, but he smothered it so she wouldn't smack him. "Have you and Ray decided about whether you want to know the sex of the baby or not?"

"We're at a stalemate. I want to know, he wants a surprise."

"I guess you could find out and just not tell him."

She shook her head. "That wouldn't work. That man can read every stinkin' thought that crosses my mind. It's some freaky Italian crystal ball shit."

He laughed. "Well, how will you know what color to paint the nursery, then?"

"Maybe just a jumble of colors. That would take care of it." She straightened up and pointed to the computer. "I guess our buddy, Pemberton, couldn't manage to keep a job until the uncle stepped in with a

116

major donation."

"With his entitled attitude, that doesn't surprise me."

"Me, either. He got shoved out at four different schools here and two others out of town before that."

"Do we know why?"

"Sounds like he finds it impossible to rein in his temper. Arguing with teachers, administration, parents…you name it. They all tried to bury the information, but the kids have online blogs yakking about it. There's even a few pictures, but they're pretty blurry."

"The one problem I have with him as a suspect is that I can't see him carefully arranging the bodies or treating them with gentleness. I think he's more the type to totally lose it. Do you agree?"

"Yup. I kinda wish it was him, though. I'd loved to slap cuffs on those pampered wrists."

"Me, too." He leaned on the edge of his desk. "How about Hatcher?"

"Nothing negative so far. No surprise that the female students think he's hot. There're even a few painfully bad poems about him online. Listen to this." She clicked a few computer keys. "I yearn from afar. He makes me want to be a star." She mimicked vomiting. "Makes me gag."

"Ah, the sheer angst of young love." He laughed. "I had a major crush on my ninth-grade teacher."

She raised an eyebrow. "Seriously?"

"Yes. Her name was Miss Spencer. Her plaid skirts and what may possibly be found under them were featured in my nightly dreams. But I kept all of the lovelorn poems to her in my head, thank goodness."

"Dork."

He smiled. "I bear the name proudly."

"How did the press conference go?"

"Same old song and dance. The bit about the date rape drug leaked somehow."

"Damn it. Oh, well. You see Pamela?"

"Yes. She walked me back."

"She and Seth seem to be making a go of it. I see them all over the neighborhood together, shopping and eating out."

"I'm glad. They're two nice people who deserve some happiness."

"Who'd have known that along with your other skills you'd be a great Cupid?" She slapped a hand on her forehead. "Speaking of which, Seth called earlier. He passed the detective's exam. Ranked third in the class."

"Oh, that's great. I thought the list came out today, but I've been too busy to check."

"So, he's off to his first assignment to get some experience, and we'll get him up here with us after he's paid his dues."

"It can't be soon enough." He changed the subject. "Did you have time to chase the Svengali emails any further?"

"There's nothing that's a hard connection yet, but something interesting came up. When I tried to trace him, the source is bounced through a lot of different dead ends. And Redding's been talking to him for a while, always about theater. So, now, I'm creeping through any deleted emails. Thank God, she never empties her wastebasket."

"So, still promising?"

"Yeah, I think your intuition is contagious. I'll keep sniffing around." They worked in silence for another two hours, then she said, "Bingo, you bastard."

He stood and joined her at her desk. "Listen to this, she got it right before she was killed. 'You are made for this part, young one. You will outshine every star in the sky. Meet me in the park behind your house Saturday morning at eleven. I'll have your costume, the script, and your paycheck.'" She groaned. "It's signed Svengali." Looking up at him, she moaned, "How could she have been so stupid?"

"She probably thought she was so close to home, what harm could it do. Damn it. He also suggested she leave her purse and phone at home since they were so close. She walked into a trap. That park has a lot of different exits which made his job easy." He rubbed his face in frustration. "Apparently, Katy Byzinski's uncle paid for her schooling, but nothing else. According to him, her waitressing paid her rent, but she couldn't afford a computer. Instead, she used that cybercafé from time to time. Let's see if we can find an email account and see if she has the same kind of mail."

Long past dinner time, they finally gave up working for the day. He drove Sanchez home. When they arrived in front of the building, he asked her to sit for a few minutes and told her about his possible advancement. As expected, she swore at him, and he waited until the string of curses ran down. "It's not definite. I just wanted to give you a heads-up."

She growled, her expression menacing. "They'd be idiots to pick anyone but you."

"You're prejudiced."

"Hey, don't talk to a Hispanic chick about

119

prejudice. We wrote the book on the subject."

"Still, you know the politics involved. It's not a sure thing until I pass all the relevant hurdles and the paper's signed."

She sighed. "Let's face it, pal, you're perfect for it. I just don't want to have to put up with another idiot partner."

He explained his plan about Seth. "If it works out, he'll be the perfect partner for you."

"You're the perfect partner for me. You spoiled me for anyone else." She tapped her fingers on the console. "But, yeah, if I can't have you, Seth is the next best thing. He's hard-working and easy to get along with."

"And he won't expect you to kowtow to him. He likes being around strong women."

"I know." She looked at him, struggling to smile. "Everything's changing."

"Yes, but change can be good."

"I guess." Tapping him on the back of his hand, she undid her seatbelt. "See you tomorrow."

"I'll be there." He waited until she was safely inside and then pulled away.

****

Later that night, Sanchez and Ray were relaxing while he cooked dinner and she told him the news. "You're kidding. I didn't know he wanted a job in administration. You guys have the best solve rate in the department, don't you?"

"Yeah, mostly because of him."

"What, are you nuts? You're a team. If he heard you spewing such bullshit, he'd kick your ass." When he peered closer at her, she made a face.

"I'm going to have to break in a new partner."

"He doesn't have the job yet."

"Give me a break. You know he's a sure thing."

He gave a good-natured shrug. "Probably, but there's gotta be some good cop around to partner besides him, right?"

She told him about the plan involving Seth. His expression darkened. "I'm not crazy about you working with someone that good-looking."

Surprised, she choked out a laugh. "Seriously? I don't think Seth is going to give up Princess Pamela for me. Besides, you were never jealous about Elijah."

"That's because he's, you know, true blue. I bet he's never cheated on a girl in his life. Besides, he's like your brother."

She thought about it for a minute. "I never had a brother, but, it's weird. If I had, I would want it to be him. I mean, he's a little too pale, but whatever." A tear came to her eye, and she shook it determinedly away. "Mother of Mary, I wish these damn hormones would quit."

"Stop worrying. You'll have the baby, he'll get the promotion, and it'll all work out."

She grumbled. "Who are you, little Suzy Sunshine? Let me bitch for a while and get it outta my system."

"Fair enough." He listened as he should, and sooner or later, she gave it up and they ate their late supper.

****

Tired and discouraged about the case, Elijah sat at his kitchen bar, forcing down a dry sandwich for dinner. As he contemplated a beer, his phone rang. This time a girl had been found on a bench on the campus of one of the local art colleges. His pipedream of beating

121

the killer to the next victim died. "Twenty minutes," he told the dispatcher as he stood, grabbing his gun, shield and a jacket. These cases were coming so close together, they could barely keep up with the workload. He texted Sanchez as he left, locking the door behind him. She agreed to meet him on the sidewalk in front of her place.

As he pulled up five minutes later, Ray bent to kiss Sanchez on the cheek and waved to Elijah. They left him standing on the pavement, looking after them.

"What a worrywart," she sighed. "Ever since I got pregnant, he acts like I'm made of glass or something. He should know better by now. If I'm glass, I'm the bulletproof variety."

"He's trying to protect his family."

"I know. It just takes some getting used to, you know what I mean."

"I do, actually. Having Dayle around makes me consider the future and what that might look like."

"You finally found yourself a keeper."

"I think you're right."

"Well, enough of all the love crap. What we got goin' on?"

"University police found a woman's body on a bench at the art college. Looks like one of ours. A few patrolmen are holding it for us."

"Oh, jeez, there're gonna be kids with cameras all over the damn place. It'll be smeared all over social media."

"Afraid so."

Their premonition was correct. The crowds that had gathered were slow to move out of the way. Things were getting out of hand. "Call and tell them we need more hands on deck," he asked Sanchez as he maneuvered as close as he could. They climbed out and the rising tide of noise overwhelmed them. The few news people who had beat them there shouted questions which they ignored.

They paused outside the crime scene tape to tell the patrolman more help had been summoned. Ducking under the tape, they went another twenty feet to where campus security waited along with another cop. "Who was the first on scene?"

The burlier of the two campus cops came forward. "That was me, Detective. Name's Harold Powers."

"When did you find our victim, Powers?"

"I found her at 8:40. Thought she'd fallen asleep, so I tapped her on the arm. She slid over on one side, so I took her pulse, found none, and called it in."

"Did you touch anything other than her arm and her neck?"

"No, detective. And I kept everyone else back, too."

"Good. You don't recognize her by any chance?"

"Seen her around a few times walking to class, but I don't know her name."

"Okay, thanks. Your partner can go back and help with crowd control, but I need you to stick around."

"I'll stay right here."

"Thanks." He and Sanchez turned and approached the scene. A young, brunette woman slumped over to one side on the bench. Her long skirt went well past her knees and stayed tucked under her legs. Her demure white blouse remained fastened. Bright red, sparkling shoes that seemed a little out of place completed her ensemble.

"Look." Sanchez gestured to one of her hands which had been draped next to three small figures. On closer inspection, they saw the figure of a shiny silver woodsman carrying an ax over one shoulder. Next to him lay a scarecrow with tufts of straw sticking everywhere. The third was a stuffed lion. Straightening, she said, "Yup. She's one of ours."

Dr. Levant pushed her way through the crowd, frowning. "This is starting to feel like deja vu," she muttered, squatting down for a look. "Poor thing." Straightening, she said, "Give me a little space, and let's see what we can find out."

Since the crime scene team had followed her, they moved back so everyone could do their jobs. Dr. Levant rejoined them first. "She's only been dead about ninety minutes. No sign of her fighting back, so it'll likely be poison or whatever again. The techs found a wallet in her purse, so you'll have her identification in a minute." She sighed. "I'll do her autopsy first thing in the morning."

"Thanks, Doc. Sorry for disturbing your evening."

She smiled. "Well, if we wanted to work nine to five, we picked the wrong business, didn't we?"

"That's certainly true." A technician brought him the victim's wallet and let him take a picture of her driver's license. Returning it to him, he watched as the morgue techs wheeled the body to the van. The medical examiner followed it off the property.

He studied his phone. "Her name is Nelly Spinks, age twenty. She lives in offsite student housing a few minutes away."

"Want to head there now?"

"Yes. We have to get ahead of this guy. There's

enough officers to help now that the others can canvass the crowd. Let's ask about security cameras, see if we can find anything there, then we'll head to her place."

There were several security cameras nearby and one of them caught the scene, but, after running it, they agreed it wasn't much help. Highly pixilated, it showed a plain white van, no license plate, backing up to a nearby corner. After a moment, a man in a black hoodie and baggy pants exited, his face concealed by a plain mask. He removed the body from the vehicle, making it look as if he was helping an inebriated friend. Cushioning her body with his, he settled her on the bench, posing her upright. It took mere minutes, and the camera never once caught anything helpful. After a brief check, he hustled back to the van, hopped in, and drove away. It had entered from the east side of the cams and exited the same way. Not much help as there were thousands of vehicles like it in the city. Two other cameras caught the van coming and going, but nothing more. They would track his route on other cameras as time went on, but that would have to wait for now.

They easily located their victim's residence. It could have passed for any older buildings that housed college students in Anywhere, USA. It was an aged, red brick foursquare, probably built, post war, in the forties. The cracked cement sidewalk had seen better days. A few beer cans and a used condom littered the lawn that had little grass which had survived the previous year's harsh summer. They swung open the exterior door, pausing to read the mailboxes and find out where they might find the manager. The rectangular tag on apartment number four's slot read "Manager." Easy to find, it was the first door on the left. They could smell the pungent odor of marijuana seeping under the door. The sound of a television blared from inside.

They had to knock twice before the sound of shuffling footsteps headed their way. The door swung open, revealing a young man in baggy, fluorescent yellow pajama pants and not much else. A few scraggly hairs adorned his bare chest. His body odor mixed with the smoke that trailed after him. He looked up and ran a clawed hand through long, black, greasy hair. "Help ya?"

"Are you the manager?" Elijah asked.

He yawned as he nodded. "Whassup?"

Elijah pulled identification and the other man straightened, an edge of trepidation lining his face. "Anything wrong?"

Sanchez snorted. "Don't care about the weed, chump. Does Nelly Spinks live here?"

"Yup. Second floor, number eight. Something wrongs with Nells?"

She raised an eyebrow. "The two of you an item?"

"Nah. She's into nerds. Do I look like a nerd to you?" He chuckled. "We're just friends. Nothing's wrong, right? I just saw her a few hours ago."

"Was she by herself?"

"Yup."

"Do you know where she was headed?"

"She just said for an adventure that would make her a few bucks." Now, he frowned, his eyes finally focused. "She's okay, then, right?"

"I'm afraid Ms. Spinks was found dead a while ago at the university."

His eyes bugged out. "No friggin' way." He leaned against the doorway. "Are you shittin' me?"

"I'm afraid not."

"How?"

"We don't know yet." After obtaining a key for her apartment, they gave him a business card and let him go back inside, still muttering under his breath. There was no elevator, so they climbed the stairs, their shoes making a muted thump on the scarred linoleum. When they found the right door, the key rattled around in the lock, but finally opened. The living room inside was a mess, but it looked like the mess of a typical college kid instead of a burglary. Empty beer cans and a few wine bottles sat in a corner and a half-eaten bag of chips lay open on the coffee table. Two rumpled blouses had been discarded on the old, flowered sofa. The room smelled repellant, like stale beer mixed with room freshener.

They moved inside, closing the door behind them. The scuffed, wooden floors creaked as they crossed the room. A few books made a haphazard stack on a small table near the tiny kitchen. He slipped on some gloves, handing a pair to his partner and flicked one open. "She's a theater student."

"Bingo," Sanchez replied. "I'd say we're on the right track." She roamed ahead of him, heading for the bedroom. Stepping inside to scan it, she said, "I don't see a laptop, though."

"Maybe she does her homework on another device. A laptop may not be essential for a theater student."

"True."

Her little bedroom contained just a messy bed and a cramped closet. A few photographs had been tacked to a small bulletin board next to her bed. They showed a few people, wearing costumes, on a stage. Sanchez snapped copies with her phone. "She's performing in these. Let's see if we can identify any of the other actors."

"Good idea."

"We'll get crime scene started on this next. You never know what they might find."

He made the necessary call. They waited until the first team member showed up, then left them to their work. Back at the precinct, they took care of the usual post-death details. Their victim's parents lived in Nevada. The local police agreed to make notification in person to spare the parents of the horror of this kind of phone call. Nelly had been a good student, well-liked, and had a terrific class average. A look at her cell phone they found beside her bed revealed similar emails from Svengali to what the other two victims had received.

Around suppertime, the phone rang with Dr. Levant on the other end. She didn't even bother responding to his greeting. "I'm going to stay and take care of your victim tonight if you can spare a hand to help."

"I appreciate it, and yes, I'd be glad to."

"I did have a brief look, and she has the same needle mark as the other two. We are probably looking at some type of poison."

"Thanks. When do you plan to start?"

"In an hour work for you?"

"I'll be there." He was grateful that, as hard as the morgue folks worked, they still understood that some cases needed priority. Explaining about the autopsy, he called and had some sandwiches delivered for them from the local deli. He just had time to eat one with a bottle of water. Glancing at his watch, he said, "I'll be back in a while." He decided to walk to clear his head. As soon as he reached the sidewalk, he got an itch on the back of his neck, what usually happened when he was being watched. He scanned from side to side as he continued, using the reflection in nearby glass windows to assist him, but didn't see anything to bother him. Getting paranoid in my old age, he thought, shaking his head. At the corner, he turned and headed to the neat red brick building. He nodded to the security guard and paused to sign in at the front desk.

He stopped just inside the swinging doors. A neat table of gowns sat there along with a clothing rack. He hung up his jacket and donned one as sixties Motown tunes starting playing softly in the background. Dr. Levant had diverse taste in music that, thankfully, didn't run to acid rock, music he despised. Right on time, she emerged from the storage rooms doors and rolled the gurney holding the body under the lights, switching them on. Pulling on a fresh set of gloves, she said, "Hi, Detective Black. Punctual as always, I see."

"Yes. I'm anxious to see what we find."

"Always happy to perform for an appreciative audience." She crossed to the autopsy table, and he followed. Never one to waste time, she spoke into the voice-activated recorder, giving the day's date and their names, including the victim's. Beginning at the deceased's head, she took painstaking note of her freckled skin along with fingers and toenails in particular. "No indication the victim fought back, no broken nails, dirt. In fact, she appears to have just had a manicure and pedicure shortly before the crime. They are in lovely shape." She took scrapings anyway in case they yielded an unseen clue. Grabbing a magnifying glass from the tray, she peered between the big toe and the one next to it. "There we are." She straightened, handing the utensil to him. "Have a look." He strained, changing the angle several times in the attempt.

"I don't see a thing."

"Well, that at least makes me feel better for having missed it the first time. It's almost invisible because it's so deep in the crease." She took her time searching, not finding anything else that would give them more. "Let's turn her over." He helped her, so that she could examine her back with the same determined skill. "I'm not seeing anything beyond that tiny prick. We'll have to rely on her blood results to help us." They laid her on her back.

He watched, frustrated at the lack of evidence, as she cut the long Y incision and opened her up. Painstakingly weighing the organs took a while. She measured each one, still murmuring. "She was a healthy young woman. Organs all reflect that. No irregularities." Sighing, she looked up. "I'm sorry, Detective. There's nothing helpful here. This guy is pretty smart. He's not leaving anything but that damn needle prick behind."

"I appreciate the extra effort, Doc." He stepped away from the table and pulled off the rumpled gown. Balling it up, he fired it into the dirty linen receptacle and stripped off his gloves. He dropped them into a nearby garbage bucket and left. Discipline kept him from asking if the blood tests were in on the two previous victims. If they had come in, she would have told him.

He was just preparing to leave after another exhausting day, having already sent Sanchez home, when his phone rang. When he saw it was Levant calling, he crossed his fingers for luck. Instead of hello, he said, "Did you find it?"

"Hell, yes," she mumbled, sounding burnt out and exhilarated at the same time. "One of the guys stayed overtime to finish getting us the results. It's snake venom."

He never saw that coming. "Are you serious?"

"Yes, believe it or not, I am. Rattlesnake venom, to be precise. The high numbers are approximately the same for the first two victims."

"How in hell would he purchase that?"

"I knew you'd ask, so I talked to a friend who's a snake lover to make sure I got my facts straight. Apparently, if you know what you're doing, snakes can be milked for their venom. After that, it's like any liquid, it can easily go into a needle."

"That means the killer we're looking for has some education in snakes. Let's hope he likes to brag. I'll get Sanchez on it first thing in the morning. You're a lifesaver."

"Thanks, Detective."

He had a moment to wish they'd got the information in time to save the Spinks girl, but they'd run with this new information now.

Chapter Twelve

The killer whistled a happy tune, more than happy with his plans for his next ingenue. She even lived conveniently close to his own home which was more than he could have asked.

Like all of them, she was young and naïve. In fact, this one was still a teenager. Being easily led into his creations proved essential.

He fed his babies as he made plans, dropping mice into their hungry, gaping mouths. The twelve reptile cages were kept tightly closed when he wasn't around. There was no need to panic the neighbors. Three of his exotics were supposed to be kept away from residences, but he knew what he was doing.

It's too bad he hadn't been able to come up with a children's book that involved snakes. It would have been a way to combine his two greatest pleasures. Instead, he referred to the stories his mother had read him. He'd kept the little books all these years and savored them still. No matter what those naysayers thought, they would have all made excellent plays.

And they would certainly be famous once again, wouldn't they? All thanks to him and his performances.

****

Late in the afternoon, the phone rang just as Elijah settled at his desk. Picking it up, he said, "Detective

Black."

"Detective, it's Victor Mann. I hope I'm not disturbing you."

"Not at all, Victor. How can I help you?"

"Well, I hope, dear man, that it might be a question of how I can help you. I had a drink last night with an old friend. He's in the business, of course, a retired Broadway actor of some note. Anyway, he reminded me of something I thought you should know."

"Any help is much appreciated."

"We had a chat about your visit because he has a better memory than I do. I thought he might remember something I didn't. He recalled a man some years ago who used to make the rounds of the small local theaters, trying to interest them in a new interpretation of children's books. I'm afraid I'd forgotten. He wasn't a teacher which was why your questions didn't ring a bell."

"How long ago was this?"

"My friend said it was about twelve years ago. His partner was dying at the time and he told him the story to make him laugh. Apparently, the man was quite convinced he should be lauded for his innovative thinking. Instead, he was scorned for the banality of his ideas."

"I don't suppose he could recall his name?"

"By some miracle, he could. His name was Andrew Middleton. He embarrassed himself by often saying it sounded like the perfect director's name."

"So, he didn't want to be an actor. He was focused on the director's role."

"Yes, apparently obsessively so. Does this information help you at all?"

Intuition raised an alarm, tensing his neck muscles. "It's a tremendous help. We'll start researching him right away. If you remember anything else, please let me know at once. And I'd appreciate you keeping the information just between you, your friend, and us."

"Of course. Happy hunting."

When Sanchez returned from the ladies' room, he said. "Victor called. We've got a solid lead." He took a few minutes to explain what their source had discovered.

"That feels like a good fit, doesn't it? Let's see what we can find on him."

"Especially if he has anything to do with snakes." What she called his spidey sense tickled the back of his neck.

She eased herself, baby belly and all, behind the desk. He waited, impatiently, as her fingers did their thing. "Andrew Middleton...hmmm. Here's a sixteen-year-old. That's not him." She gave a huff. "Here we go. Age forty-five, unmarried, five-foot-ten, black hair that looks dyed, stringy mustache. Prints theater programs for a living." She turned the screen towards him. "This guy's smile's as fake as a six-dollar bill. Wouldn't the girls' creep radar have gone off?"

"We both know from long experience that not everyone has creep radar like we do."

"It should be a Christmas present for every teenager on the planet." She kept looking. "Let's see what we can dig up on social media."

"Do a quick run, then dig up an address for him and saddle up. After I fill the lieutenant in, let's have a look at his place and see if we can get a peek at him. If he works regular nine to five hours, he could possibly be returning home soon."

"Yup."

While she gathered the information, he found his boss by himself and filled him in on the break. "Yesterday, we didn't have anything substantial on this guy, but, you're right, this feels solid," Porter replied. "Let's get some eyes on him, starting with you guys tonight. It might have to come down to catching him in the act. See if Sanchez can find anything in the emails that might help."

"Yes, sir."

"Stay alert."

When he returned to the office to grab his partner, he found her staring at the computer. When she heard his approaching steps, she looked up, glee stretching her face with a grin. "You're gonna freakin' flip."

"Did you find something?"

"I just struck the damn mother lode. Guess what this dude does in his spare time?"

He just waited.

"He's a damn herpetologist." She stumbled a little over the term. "Didn't graduate, but he's plenty trained in dealing with poisonous snakes. There're at least a dozen pictures on social media. One of them is showing him milking his snake of venom." She grinned. "And guess what he listed as the only thing he loves more than snakes?"

"The theater?" he said hopefully.

"Give the man a gold star."

Relief flooded him. "It's him."

"Damn right, it's him. Let's go figure out how to trap the sonofabitch."

An hour later, they were seated in the car across

from a small, crumbling brick bungalow in a borderline safe neighborhood. Although it was dinnertime, they had seen no signs of life anywhere near the house, thus far. Sanchez munched on a cookie and offered the bag to him. He took two to keep his stomach from rumbling and handed the bag back. "Does this look like the home of a successful director to you?" she joked.

"I think he's delusional at best. Maybe he's huffed too many odors from printer's ink."

"I just hope I don't have to go anywhere near the inside of that house." She shivered. "How much do you bet they're crawlin' all over the damn place?"

"Don't you worry. We're not letting baby anywhere near that building."

They settled in for a wait, but it didn't take long. Thirty minutes later, a man came strolling down the broken sidewalk, a cheery whistle sounding in time with his steps. Dressed all in black, he looked more like a funeral director than a printer. A flamboyant red tie was the only nod to fashion. His smile looked painted on, like a creepy clown, his mustache mirroring the unnatural lift of his lips. As expected, he entered the driveway, went up the walk and let himself into the house with a key pulled from his pocket. "He looks like a cartoon character," Sanchez said, rolling her eyes. "How much do ya bet he started out as a frustrated actor?"

"Could be." After a few minutes with no further sign of activity, Elijah told his partner to grab a nap. Ninety minutes passed. Just when he thought the man might be retiring for the night, the door opened again. He woke Sanchez. They both observed as he went to the garage out back, opening the big door to reveal a car.

"I wonder if it's registered. It didn't show up on any search." As it rolled past them, they saw an old license plate, mostly covered in mud. "Oldest trick in the book," she murmured. "He's not as smart as he thinks."

They lagged a few cars back as they followed, intent on staying below the radar, taking their time. He didn't travel far. Two neighborhoods away, he turned in and took the first street to the right. They took a chance and moved closer to see what he was doing. Cruising down the street, his car slowed to a crawl as he passed one house in particular. They watched as he looked at the windows with the curtains drawn. His head swiveled as he checked out the driveway and the sole car parked there, a dark blue, four-door sedan. They dropped back and followed from a safe distance as he cruised all the streets around the house. "Got the address down?" he asked as he drove.

"Yup. I'm searching for particulars on the home owners."

"He's cased every detail. Now it looks like he's headed home."

Sanchez hummed as she searched. "According to the property records, the house belongs to Fred and Althea Dunn. She's a music teacher. He's an engineer." She cursed. "Two kids—one's a teenage girl. Name's Rebecca. She's a senior and, judging by her social media, she loves her theater classes."

"He's not going to take her tonight. He's in planning mode. We'll keep eyes on him and, this time, we'll get him before he claims another one." They pulled over at the corner of his street and watched as he garaged the car and returned to the house. After a short wait, all of the interior lights went off.

"Looks like it's bedtime." Elijah called one of the nearby patrolmen to take Sanchez home to Ray. She bitched about it until he said he'd need her to help set up the trap the next day and baby needed rest. After that reassurance, she left willingly. As he settled back on Middleton's street, slouched against the head rest for comfort, he texted Ray to let him know she was on the way home. He and his friend had a private agreement. He would always keep a special eye out for Sanchez and the baby. That would be priority one, at least for now.

Elijah texted Dayle to keep her apprised of the stakeout, and she answered before heading to bed. As expected, everything stayed quiet all night. He ignored his complaining stomach and followed their suspect to the print shop where he worked in the morning. The uninspiring square brick building offered little in roadside appeal other than a freshly painted door and a new sign. After checking it out, he ran home to shower and get into some clothes that didn't smell like body odor and frustration. He grabbed a to-go cup of coffee, ate a bagel, and kissed Dayle. After ascertaining that everything was okay with her, he returned to the precinct.

Sanchez showed up, well-rested, but with a frown marring her expression. "What's this alpha male bullshit about me not sitting on a stakeout?"

"Babies need rest. It's more important to have your help today."

"Oh, all right," she said, rolling her eyes. "How do you want to handle it?"

"We need to put this together fast. If he was cruising by the house, it might be a final check before he acts. I don't want us anywhere near the Dunns' house. He might be watching it on his lunch hour or even coffee breaks if he's getting close to carrying out the grab."

"That makes sense to me."

"Can you find out any additional information on the family that might help? Have either of them had issues with police in the past, that kind of thing. After that, I'd say we get the parents in here, tell them what's going on, and whisk the kids out of there for safekeeping. They can't make a big production out of it, though, or he'll know somethings up."

"We need a dive into the girl's computer."

He considered for a moment. "If it's a laptop, one of the parents can smuggle it out of the house and we can see what's on it."

"If they let us."

"I'd say of course they will, but you never know how people are going to react to something like this."

"You want me to clear it with Porter and set it up while you hammer down on the emails for the first three victims?"

"That works for me."

The conversation with his lieutenant was quick and to the point. He was thrilled they finally had some actionable information and told him to continue round the clock surveillance on the suspect and set up the sting asap.

On returning to the office, Elijah located the father at his job. As calmly as he could, he informed him, in rather vague terms, of the potential threat. It wouldn't be wise to panic him at this stage. The man's first instinct, after his initial curious response, was to proclaim that his daughter would never interact with a stranger on the Internet. *How many times have I heard that one?* Eventually, he agreed to come with his wife to the precinct with the laptop in question to, as he put it, clear all of this up. They were advised that someone might be watching the house and to act as normal as possible.

When the parents showed up an hour later, righteous indignation had taken hold. The father entered like a bantam rooster, puffing out his chest and stretching his five-foot-eight to look as forbidding as he could manage. "I don't appreciate all of this drama over nothing. It's clearly a waste of our time to come here." He shoved a clawed hand through his short, brown hair.

Elijah paused to introduce himself and his partner. "I hope you're correct and this is a false alarm." He waved them to their seats across from him. "However, what I didn't want to tell you on the phone was this. Last night, the suspect was seen casing your house and examining all of the streets around your property." The man's jaw dropped and his wife started to cry, swiping long, bleached blonde hair out of her eyes.

"We followed him from his house, and he examined all the exits to and from your home. I'm sure that clarifies for you the reason for our concern."

Now, they clutched hands so hard the skin of their fingers rimmed with white. Without another word, Mr. Dunn opened his briefcase, his hands shaking, and removed the laptop they'd brought. Elijah took it and passed it to Sanchez. "Thank you," Elijah said. "While we're talking, with your permission, my partner is going to search your daughter's incoming emails."

"O-of course." After he handed the laptop over, the mother provided her password which was painfully easy to hack—Rebecca 1234. They had to strain to hear her subdued voice.

He made an effort to relax back in his seat, trying to keep the parents calm. "Now, does Rebecca enjoy the theater classes she takes at school? Her social media seemed to indicate that she did."

"Yes, she does," Fred answered, his lips turning downward. "I think they're a little ridiculous myself, but she's a good student, so I guess it's okay to have one fluff class."

"Is that how she thinks of it? As a fluff class?"

He chuckled with disdain rather than humor. "Oh, no, you'd think she was headed straight for Broadway the way she carries on. Now, she's talking about majoring in it in university." Huffing, he added, "As I told her mother, she can pay for it herself, then."

Sanchez's voice broke in. "Found 'em, Elijah."

He looked up, ignoring their confused reactions. "How bad?"

"The worst. He plans to meet her tonight."

Frantic at the news, her parents begged to know what was going on, their looks bouncing from one partner to the other. "There's no need to panic," he soothed, putting a hand out to stop their babbled questions. "We will take you to Rebecca's school right now. You can pick both of your children up and return here until we determine it's safe to return."

"He'll get away with it," the mother cried.

"No, we'll set a trap for him, but we have to move quickly."

"What kind of a trap?" Now, Dad was fully on board.

"We'll use a decoy instead of your daughter. But first things first. We will send you to each child's school with a plainclothes officer to remove your children and bring them here. Please tell them nothing until you get back to this office."

"Our son, too? Why?"

"It's essential to use an abundance of caution in cases like this. Sometimes, if a suspect can't get the original target, they'll settle for the next best thing."

The woman looked like she was going to faint, and Sanchez scurried to bring her a glass of water. After a small drink, she whispered, "Thanks," and some color returned to her cheeks.

The two men they'd requested showed up at the door. "They'll take you safely to and from both schools. Simply go to the principal's office, say you have a family emergency, and sign them out. Tell them nothing more until you're all back here, and don't let them use their phones."

Fred nodded, gathering his wife to his side. "We'll be back as soon as we can."

After they had disappeared through the doors, Sanchez said, "They're clean as a whistle. A few parking tickets, that's all. Both kids are on the honor roll at school."

"Okay. What's the physical description on the daughter?"

"Five foot six, dark brown hair to the shoulders, blue eyes. Curvy."

"Are we sure that's current?"

"Lucky for us, she posts on social media every day.

A selfie from last night confirms it."

"Let's do a search for a policewoman who fits, someone who looks young enough to pull it off." He worked on other details as she searched. He heard an expression of surprise and paused. "What?"

"I think we found the perfect girl, but jeez, she looks like she really should be in high school."

He wandered to her desk to look over her shoulder. "Well, that makes me feel ancient, but she's perfect. How soon can we get her in here?"

"She's on the beat today, so it shouldn't be a problem. Only been on the job for five months, though."

"I'm not worried about that. She'll be wearing a vest, and we'll cover her like a blanket. Get her in here asap."

She made the necessary calls in short order, barking, "Got it. She'll be here within the hour."

Chapter Thirteen

Elijah paced around the room, ignoring everyone but Sanchez. They had to get every detail right or lives could be at stake, especially that of their undercover bait. "What's her name again?" he asked, pausing to face her.

"Cheryl Pope. So, what else can we take care of until she shows up?"

"Let's work out the hiding places for the other officers. We can get her up to speed when she shows. It shouldn't be long now."

"Which location is he trying to lure her to?"

He thought better when he moved and, so, began to pace again. "Her high school, which presents quite a challenge. The main building has a lot of open parking areas around it. No trees or anything else to give our people a place to hide."

"I can get the blueprints. Just give me a minute." Her fingers on the keyboard flew. A few minutes later, she said, "Here we go. You better look. I can't read these things worth a damn."

He nodded, peering over her shoulder. "Okay, this doesn't look too bad."

"How many entrances in the building?"

"Six, but only two of them are main entrances." He pointed to show her. "The other four are just single doors off the rear parking lot." He swung around to stand, facing her. "Now, if you're an organized killer, where would you have her meet you?"

"Less likely to be seen in the back lot. Not as many security lights, either, which is dumb. Should be the other way around with extra lighting in the back."

He smirked. "Guess where one of the back doors leads?"

"The theater department?"

"Even better. The stage."

Her eyes bugged out. "Ya think he's gonna try and lure her onto the stage to kill her there?"

He could see every step of it in that man's psychotic mind. "It's upping his game, right? He always wanted to be taken seriously, be a member of the theater community. If I was a betting man, I'd lay stakes on it."

"How would he get in? If he breaks down the door, he'll set off the alarm."

"That, I don't know. I would bet he's either stolen a key or paid someone off to leave the door open. We also have to have enough people that if he tries to grab her from the parking lot instead, we can still get to her in time."

She scrunched her face, deep in thought. "So, how many cops? Too many and he's bound to get suspicious or someone screws up. Maybe one for each door and another six to cover the stage and surrounding areas?"

"A dozen warm bodies, plus our decoy. Sounds about right." Another thought made him frown. "Our best guess is that he delivers the venom in a syringe. Maybe multiple syringes since the needles are small. When would he be likely to give it to her?"

"Anytime between the door and arriving at the stage, probably."

"That's where the biggest risk is. Let's say, they enter the door at the top center position. They have to pass all of those seats in the audience before they arrive at the stage where the next level of protection is waiting. What if he pauses on the way and tries to stick her with a needle?" Immediately, he shook his head, angry at himself for not thinking of one fact. "Now, wait. He's been sticking them between the toes and I think he'll stay on script and continue on the same way. So, he'll have to dose her first, maybe offer her a drink on the way in, but not administer the venom until they reach the stage where he can convince her to lie down."

They stayed quiet, thinking it through. "We still have to cover every eventuality," Sanchez said. "He's not going to look down every row in the audience, right? He'll be focused getting her to the stage." Her eyes lit with an idea. "Why don't we have two officers halfway down the rows, lying on the floor? They'd be close enough to get to her quickly if needed."

"That would probably work. After they enter the building, the excess officers that weren't needed outside can cover the front hall outside the theater doors. That way, we can box him in of necessary."

"Yeah. If she has to take a drink, it's not the end of the world, but we can't let him get that needle anywhere near her."

"Exactly." He paused. "Let's get an ambulance to wait nearby with some anti-venom. Better safe than sorry."

"Okay. I'll check out the nearest zoo with a snake exhibit. I'm sure they'll have some."

They were interrupted by a brisk rap on the open door. A slender woman of medium height stood waiting, her bright eyes now familiar from her online picture. "Officer Pope, reporting for assignment. Are you Detectives Black and Sanchez?"

"Yes," they answered in tandem. She entered, enthusiasm showing in the ready smile she offered. Her petite figure and brown hair made her an excellent match for their would-be victim. They sat down with her and explained the case thus far, as well as their plans.

"Well, that's a coincidence," she replied. "Guess where I went to high school?"

The fact that she was familiar with the footprint of the school made him happier with their plan. "You'll be in a vest, of course. We don't expect overt violence from this guy, but we are always prepared for it. So far, as far as we can determine, his MO has been to give a drink laced with GHB, then inject snake venom. So, no matter what, don't get close enough that he can stick you. Keep an eye on his hands. The medical examiner told us he would need a relatively large amount to administer enough to kill, so he can't easily make a subtle approach. At best guess, it will be multiple small syringes hidden somewhere on his person or in something he carries. We will have you well-surrounded with officers, anyway."

"Yes, sir. I'm very quick on my feet, so I'm not worried."

When the family were suddenly hustled through the doors, he waved them to a group of chairs they'd arranged at the back of the conference room. After they were settled, he left Sanchez figuring out how to dress their decoy with a selection of clothes offered by female staff.

Sitting down to explain the problem they were facing, the daughter, Rebecca, was defensive until the reality of her situation was revealed to her. She gasped, then she started sobbing, blubbering out an explanation. "He was really nice to me. He said he'd seen a few of our plays and thought I was the most talented one in the cast."

"We saw some of the emails from Svengali on your laptop. How long has he been in contact with you?"

"About three months." She sniffled. "He said we had to wait for the perfect project, that he'd know when the time was right."

"I know it doesn't seem like it, but you're lucky," he said, trying to console her. "You're very lucky you were his fourth choice and not his first."

"What do you mean?" In as quiet a voice as he could manage, he explained to her about the previous victims. She shook her head repeatedly. "I know he's not the guy who hurt those other girls. He can't be."

"He didn't hurt them, he killed them," her father shouted. "How could you be so stupid?"

Rebecca's cries turned into shrieks. He could have done without the father's so-called assistance. "Let's all calm down now," he murmured. "You are safe, which is the important thing." He patted her father's arm when he apologized for losing his temper. "We'll get you all some lunch and, later, dinner, and make you as comfortable as possible. Hopefully, this will all be cleared up by bedtime, and you can return to your home."

Assigning Detective Davis to watch the family, he

busied himself concocting a quick plan that would work and keep everyone safe. Especially Sanchez, who refused to keep in the background despite her baby on board. Working together, they sketched it out and made the relevant calls for backup.

Hours later, on scene, he tried to place Sanchez in the least likely doorway, but she wasn't having any part of it. "Alpha asshole," she coughed out, grimacing. "Not on your life. I'm not missing all the excitement." Instead, he positioned her on the stage with him at her insistence. To make himself feel better, he convinced Seth, who he had borrowed for the evening, to lie in the aisle closest to her so that she had extra coverage on both sides.

The lush, scarlet curtains on both sides of the stage gave them some extra coverage. They were all safely in place a full hour before the rendezvous to make sure they weren't caught off guard by any last-minute challenges. The message that Pope was ready to go had come via text. Now was the worst part—waiting. The only thing that united them were the units in their ears that transmitted whatever Cheryl Pope said. Her job was to feed them clues as she and the suspect approached, clues about their current location in and around the building that would compel the necessary response.

Each cop checked in every ten minutes until fifteen minutes before the meet. After that, everyone maintained radio silence. With three minutes to go before the deadline, he heard Cheryl say, in a light, soft voice, "Oh, there you are. I'm glad you waited by the main entrance. It's not so spooky here. Are we going inside?"

"Yes." Middleton's deep voice swelled. "After you, my dear."

Elijah imagined the officers leaving the extra posts and closing in around the building as planned. He heard the murmur of both players' voices, saying banal pleasantries as they walked. "How exciting," Pope said as they appeared at the top of the stairs. "I can't believe you were able to get the keys."

"I have friends in high places," he boasted and she gave a girlish giggle in response. Elijah watched from stage left as they entered the theater and passed the first set of cops lying between the audience seating. "You can see my vision as a director now, can't you?"

"Oh, yes. I'm so excited. I can't believe I'm getting such a wonderful opportunity."

"You deserve it." He swept an arm around in a flamboyant gesture, like a game show hostess. "This stage was meant to feature you in a way the public will never forget."

"As if I was on Broadway?" Her simpering tone fed his grandiose personality. Even Elijah felt convinced by her acting.

"This is so much better than Broadway." Arriving at the front of the theater, they moved to the side stairs in order to climb to the stage. Through a break in the curtains, Elijah's eyes met Sanchez's.

An accomplished actress of a different sort met her so-called director in the middle of the stage. The latter set down the large bag he carried. "What should we do first?" Cheryl asked. "I mean, how do we prepare for the scene?"

He crouched to pull a plastic drink container from his bag. Standing, he beamed. He handed it to her and said, "Have a drink to refresh yourself first."

She demurred with a shy smile. "Oh, I'm not thirsty, thanks. You can have it."

Elijah caught sight of the anger that flashed across his face, then was smothered. "Oh, I must insist. You must be well-hydrated for your voice to ring out with conviction. It's essential to project so that even someone seated on the back row can hear you."

She took the bottle and held it. "When can I see the script?" It was clearly an attempt to buy some time.

Clenching his teeth, he lectured her, the words bursting from him in a stern tone. "A good actress always does what her director asks. Perhaps you are too young to understand. I'm not sure that you deserve this part."

She widened her eyes in a pleading expression. "I'm so excited that if I drink now, I might get sick. That would ruin everything."

"Drink!"

Raising it to her lips, she pretended to swallow. "Mmm. That's good."

A roar of anger burst out of him, and he grabbed her. The drink tumbled to the stage, spilling everywhere. "You're ruining everything," he screamed. "I'm in charge here. I'm the director." In a flash, he snatched a knife from his pocket and held it to her throat. "Now, you'll drink it, won't you? I'll make you lick it up on all fours if I have to."

To her credit, Pope stayed still and calm in his arms. Elijah stepped out from behind the curtain, gun drawn. "NYPD," he said loudly. "Put your weapon down."

The murderer's look of surprise might have been

comical if the situation wasn't so dire. "Leave the stage," he bellowed, taking two steps back and dragging Cheryl with him. "You are the intruder here. We are in dress rehearsal."

Sanchez slipped out of her hiding place, not four feet behind the killer. She eased up silently as he took another step back. Screwing her gun against the back of his neck, she warned, "Drop the knife, or you'll have a large, gaping hole where your head used to be."

He wavered, loosening his arm, and Pope flopped down to the floor, out of his grasp. At the same time, Elijah leapt forward and squeezed his wrist until he dropped the knife. Sanchez took a step back, her gun trained on him for backup. They forced the killer onto his stomach. When Cheryl slid away to the side, out of the way, he cuffed him. "Do you know who I am?" the suspect shrieked. "I'll have you blackballed. You'll never work another day in this city."

As Elijah turned him over, then yanked him to his feet, Sanchez said. "Yeah, I know who you are, asshole. You're Mr. Friggin' Delusional. Nice to meet you." Barely containing a laugh, she waited as Elijah organized the suspect's removal. The others had all gathered to help. Seth and another officer marched Middleton out to a waiting patrol car. "Good job," Sanchez said to Cheryl, giving her a hand off the floor. "You'd never know you're in your first year. You did great."

"Thanks, Detective," she said, glowing as she brushed off her pants. "I hope to be a detective someday."

"We'll be proud to have you."

The half-empty bottle of dosed water was put into

an evidence bag to be tested, along with the knife. They closed things down in record time. It felt great to subdue a suspect with no injuries on anyone, not even a scratch. After they drove back to the precinct to file reports, they allowed the exhausted Dunn family to go home. Filling out the paperwork took two hours. Ray showed up to get his wife, so Elijah headed straight home to Dayle. She opened the door with a knowing smile. "Got him?"

"Yes, ma'am." He gave a tired sigh and followed her inside. Not for the first time, he relished the fact that he had such a wonderful woman to greet him at night.

"I'll bet Lieutenant Porter was happy to get a case like this solved somewhat quickly. Did the guy admit to the other killings?"

"No. He was too busy promising we were all going to lose our jobs because of his standing in the theater community. His delusions are out of control."

"Do you think he'll try for an insanity defense?"

"Probably. And this time, it might actually have some substance."

Dayle made him a sandwich, sitting at the table to keep him company as he ate. He told her the story from beginning to end. Not long after, they retired to bed early, knowing that the press would have a field day tomorrow with the case being closed.

Chapter Fourteen

Elijah never told Sanchez much about their search of Middleton's house. What they'd found gave him snake nightmares for a night or two, and he knew it would have been worse for her. These days, all her dreams were about everything threatening her baby. He, along with other officers and animal control, had found fifteen reptiles, most of them huge and poisonous, living in stacked reptile cages in his living room. He had watched, from a safe distance, as they were carefully collected and taken to vans for transport. The neighbors had observed, aghast, from the yard next door. He imagined that having such danger nearby gave them second thoughts about their safety.

In the master bedroom, they'd found a room more like one that belonged to a child. In one corner, children's books were stacked, along with a few stuffed toys from characters within the tales. There was also a framed picture showing an older woman with the word Mama on her shirt. Hanging on the wall was a picture of Middleton wearing a matching shirt that said, Director. On a shelf next to it was a cheap fake trophy that spelled out Best Director in peeling, gold letters. It creeped out everyone at the scene, setting a new, dubious standard to beat. They also found photographs of small shows featuring his snakes. At some point, his desire for a real audience had led him to a destiny of horror.

As Elijah wrapped up the evidence gathering at the house, he reflected on the other good news he'd heard. Detective Hadley had accepted a new posting in Burglary and was leaving by the end of the week. To say that everyone else was thrilled was an understatement. Even his partner, Davis, smiled a little more these days.

Closing up the house, he gave a grateful sigh and headed home.

****

When Dayle had suggested a girl's night out with the two of them and Pamela Clayton, Sanchez had been shocked. She hadn't been on such an outing since high school. Women never really knew what to make of her because of her atypical job and the fact that she didn't live or die based on female niceties. She never hid her opinion or particularly cared what people thought of her. But what shocked her even more about the invitation was that she said yes.

So, on Friday night, after the latest case finally closed, all three managed to get a few hours off to themselves. They agreed to meet downtown at Lascivious, an uptown bar that catered to the professional crowd. Sanchez wondered at the name of the club, but all was answered once she stepped inside the door. As she moved aside to slide off her jacket, she paused to look at the interior. Gorgeous lingerie in every shade was featured on the walls, highlighted with spotlights. Low, throbbing music played in the background. Both men and women servers wore provocative clothes that accented each person's physical attributes. What a hoot, she thought, as she scanned to find the other two women waving from a booth at the back of the room. She walked to meet her friends, glad she'd worn a dressy skirt. Even with her baby on board, she knew she looked gussied-up enough to fit in with the other customers. "Hey, you guys," she said, slipping in beside Dayle. She turned to look at Pamela. "Let me guess, you picked this place."

"Guilty as charged." Her blonde friend looked a little less doll-like these days, but still attracted more than her share of attention in a fitted white dress and long gold earrings.

Gesturing to the attached boutique, she said, "Are you picking up a few new outfits to dazzle Seth with later?"

"Maybe. How about you two?"

Sanchez gestured to her belly. "Not sure how much sexy I can carry off these days."

Dayle, blushing, looked uncomfortable. She tugged at the collar of her silk blouse. "I prefer a little more coverage, not less. My ex-husband used to love all that stuff. I guess associating it with him turned me off."

Pamela shrugged. "They have some more elegant stuff, too. Let's take a look after. If nothing else, you can help me pick something."

Dayle couldn't help teasing. "How is Seth these days?"

The news reporter beamed. "Seth is wonderful. I'll always be grateful to Elijah for introducing us. I've dated so many men, kissed a lot of frogs in this particular pond, but Seth is perfect for me. He's kind, thoughtful and, take my word for it, he's great in bed."

Sanchez pretended to gag. "All the love crap

floating around these days…you'd think you're making a commercial for a dating app."

The other two laughed. Dayle said, "Give me a break. You're the one with the Italian stallion and a baby on the way. Maybe you're the poster girl for eternal love."

"Oh, jeez. Italian stallion? Don't call him that. His head is swollen enough these days."

"Have you thought about names yet?" Pamela asked.

"Don't get me started," she said, feeling a grimace stretching her full cheeks. "One of Tony's friends suggested Diablo if it's a boy. I said, you moron, that means devil in Spanish. Why the hell would I call my kid that? You know what he said?"

They shook their heads.

"He said, 'Ah, come on, it'll be funny.'" She cursed under her breath. "What a damn meatball. It's a good thing he's good-lookin' or no sensible chick would take a second look."

"So, no names yet?"

"Nah, but we got lots of time."

"Do you know if it's a boy or a girl?"

"Yeah, but we're keeping it as a surprise."

When Dayle excused herself to head to the ladies' room, Pamela turned towards Sanchez. "I didn't want to ask, but how's the situation with Dayle's ex-husband? Elijah mentioned that he's been causing problems. I didn't want to ruin the evening by asking her."

"He's a damn freak, but we're all keeping our eyes peeled for any trouble. After getting dragged into our case last year, she doesn't need anything else bad to happen. She just moved in with Elijah, though, so she should be safer."

"Oh, I didn't know that. That's good news. So, they're serious?"

She grinned. "I haven't seen him so happy in years. I think he finally found his match."

"I'm so glad. He's a really great guy. He deserves that."

When Dayle returned, they talked about their jobs, the guys, and the baby as they ate. Before they left, they wandered through the boutique. Not only were there scads of gorgeous undies, but one corner held sex toys in myriad colors. They giggled, promising to return for a closer look and egged on Pamela, who chose two racy teddies with heat-inducing cutouts. Dayle found a soft, sheer, blue nightie that skimmed her knees. It satisfied her need for what she called her "moderately sexy" look. Even Sanchez found a short, black nightie that showed off her chest, but still had room for baby. After being called, Ray picked Sanchez up and the other two split a cab. After she climbed into the car, he asked, "So, how was your first girl's night?"

"It was fun." To her eternal surprise, it had been. Maybe now that she was a little older and married, making female friends would be easier. On paper, she and the others were very different, but being around them was a breeze.

"See, now you're pregnant, you're getting all girly on me." He beamed at the thought.

"Give me a break." She rolled her eyes. "We talked mostly about you three cavemen and work."

"What have you got in the bag?"

She waited until he was looking her way, then ran her tongue over her lips. "If you behave yourself, you might get a peek when we get home."

His eyes lightened and he picked up speed, making her laugh like a kid.

****

In thanks for all of the hard work on the case, the lieutenant gave them a well-earned and rare weekend off. Elijah made sure they spent it in quiet relaxation mode other than making short work of Dayle's move to the house. A few days ago, a neighbor had bought most of her furniture on the spot. She donated the rest to charity. Ray borrowed a small, flat trailer from one of his many relatives, and they moved all of her things to the house. It only took two hours. Elijah had made room in his closet by removing half of his clothes and moving them to the spare room. He did the same thing with his dresser. Everyone's help made the move easy and she said she felt at peace in the lovely house with its cozy ambience.

****

On Monday morning, Dayle's assistant stuck her head inside the doorway. "I have a delivery for you. Should I bring it in?"

"Sure, Sally. Thanks."

She glanced up as the other woman entered, her small hands struggling with a huge vase of gardenias. She stood and, together, they settled it on a spare table in the corner. "Is there a card?"

"Yes, ma'am." She handed her the white square plucked from between the stems. "They're beautiful." Excusing herself, she closed the door behind her. Dayle opened the card, wondering why Elijah would be so extravagant. It said *It won't be long before I see you again.*

Recognizing the handwriting, she dropped it, her heart thudding in her chest. Christopher. *Would she never find lasting peace?*

Her knees suddenly weak, she plunked into her chair with a thud. She raised trembling hands to her face. What should she do? The time seemed to tick past like an omen as she sat there, frozen. When her cellphone rang, she jumped. Picking it up and peering at the screen, she was relieved to see it showed Elijah's number. "H-hello?"

"Are you okay? You sound upset." When she didn't answer, he said, "Dayle?"

His worried words jarred her out of her funk. "I'm here."

"What's the matter?"

She took a calming breath. "He sent me flowers."

"Just now?"

"Yes."

"I'll be right there." The line cut off, and she lowered her phone to her lap. She stayed where she was, worried she might crumple to the floor. Hating the feeling that she was losing control, she convinced herself to calm down. In seven minutes flat, Elijah knocked and entered. He shut the door behind him. Joining her, he crouched down to rest on his heels so he could meet her gaze even as she slumped. When she looked up, he hugged her. "You're okay."

"Why does this keep happening?" She gestured to the flowers.

"Was there a note?"

She indicated where it still lay on the floor. He picked it up and read it. A rare spasm of anger crossed his face. Cursing under his breath, he rose to his full height. "Okay. I'm going to take care of the flowers and the note. We'll check and see if there are any prints. Let me arrange that, then I'm taking you home."

"I still have work."

"You can do it tomorrow. We both need to get out of here for a while."

She allowed herself to be cared for, something with which she always struggled. In no time, he had taken care of the flowers and the note, returning to hustle her out the door. The silent drive home seemed endless. Back at the brownstone, he led her to the couch and got her settled. He stayed silent, allowing her some time to let worry drain away as much as possible. Snuggling a blanket around her legs, he brewed them each a hot cup of coffee. She took a sip as he sat by her feet. "I feel like such a burden."

"That's something you could never be." He rubbed her feet and it felt like heaven. "I just think you're not used to someone taking care of you. More importantly, you should realize by now that I want the job."

She realized she had given up on finding someone to do that years ago. "Christopher cured me of relying on anyone, I guess."

He smiled. "We all have to rely on someone, now and then."

"I'm afraid I don't find it easy to trust many people."

"I'd say having a violent ex-husband would sabotage anyone's sense of safety. You think I don't understand, but I do. Since my parents died, the only person I really trust besides you is Sanchez."

"How about Ray?"

"I like Ray, but it takes time to develop true

friendship, doesn't it? He and I are working on it."

She took a breath, mortified that tears threatened. "What am I going to do?"

He set his mug down on the coffee table. "We're going to consult a few friends on how to best protect you and catch him in the act. I know your problems with him seem never-ending, but we are going to solve this problem. He's not calling the shots anymore."

In the morning, she bit the bullet and called Christopher's parole officer, Ernie Watts. He seemed to blow off the gifts and the flowers at first, then she reminded him that she was an assistant DA and not prone to over-stating things. "This was the kind of thing he did before, you see, so it's just more of the same."

"Okay, I get it. I can have a word with him when he comes in for his next appointment, but there's not much more I can do unless he ramps up to something more serious."

She blew out a frustrated breath. "You have to understand my perspective, officer. The last time the authorities didn't think it was a big deal, I ended up almost bleeding to death from a knife wound. I'm trying to exercise preventative measures."

"Oh, I get it, but my hands are tied. I'll do the best we can under the circumstances." With a subdued goodbye, she ended the call.

Dayle entered the office after a meeting and saw a single folder lying on her desk. Frowning, she wondered what she'd left behind. She opened it and saw the note, typewritten in large font.

The dutiful detective can't hide you forever. It's kind of pathetic how he hangs over you every waking moment.

I'll let you choose the way I'll get rid of him: getting ravaged by fire as his brownstone burns? Or perhaps he dies in a shootout with an unknown assailant.

There are a lot of ways for a cop to die.

Get rid of him or I'll make my choice.

The clock's ticking.

The logical part of her knew she should call Elijah. She trusted him to take care of her. She really did. Her hand reached for the phone several times and she jerked it back. She thought of all the care he'd shown her, but realized she couldn't risk his safety or that of Sanchez and her baby.

They hadn't spoken of love, but who was she kidding? He exemplified everything she wanted in a life partner—intelligence, empathy, and they shared more sexual chemistry than she'd could ever have expected. And to top it off, he made her laugh, something that had been harder to do in recent years. For a long while, she'd become so guarded that no one could break through her walls.

She yearned for a future with him, but she couldn't risk his safety. He didn't deserve to be hurt because of her choice all those years ago. Better to hurt him now and keep them all safe in the process.

Mumbling to her assistant that she'd be out for the rest of the day, she grabbed her coat and purse. Sally asked her if she was okay, looking concerned. "Yes, yes," she assured her as she hurried past, down the elevator and out on the street. It wouldn't take long to remove her things from the brownstone while he was at work. Nerves attacked her from every direction. What was she thinking? How could she have endangered the man she loved?

Chapter Fifteen

Christopher spied on her from across the busy street, grinning, as she stepped into a cab, looking frantic. *Oh, Dayle, you're so predictable. You would sacrifice yourself for the greater good as predicted. What a fool.* Stepping into his car, he followed her to Elijah's place. He wound his way to the back, parking his car in the alley.

Skulking through the back yard, he saw the light go on in the bedroom and knew she was packing in a mad rush. Keeping his guard up as he searched for nosy neighbors, he slipped to the front and waited in the nook by the front door. He clutched a cloth with chloroform in his hand.

Sure enough, ten minutes later, she opened the heavy door and backed out, dragging two cases behind her. Before she could even close the door, he snatched her hair, yanking her head back to hold the cloth over her mouth. Shoving her head away, she banged into his chin. The crack was audible, and it was almost enough to loosen his grip. But it was too late for her. She sagged to the floor. He picked her up in his arms, leaving her cases where they toppled.

Scanning the surrounding houses, he saw no one. With long strides, he carried her to the back where his car waited. He fumbled the door open and put her in the passenger seat, slamming the door behind her. Hurrying to the driver's side, he jumped in and sped away, his tires squealing on the asphalt.

****

Around noon, the desk sergeant called from the front lobby. "Black, we got a lady on the main line, saying she's your neighbor. Says it's an emergency."

He frowned at the phone. "Put her through."

A breathless voice greeted him, one he recognized. "Elijah, this is Letty, your next-door neighbor."

"Yes, Letty. Is something wrong?"

"I think a man grabbed your girlfriend and took her away."

His stomach dropped. She must be wrong. He'd accompanied Dayle to work himself. "Tell me what exactly you saw."

Sanchez sat up, looking in his direction, her eyebrows raised.

"Your lady was coming out with her suitcases, and he snatched her right up. He carried her away and left her cases behind on your porch. I watched them with my binoculars, but I couldn't do anything but call you."

"What did he look like?"

"Tall and kinda fancy, blond hair. Maybe forty years old."

His stomach lurched. "Did she fight him?"

"No. She walked backwards out the door, dragging her cases, but then she slumped over after he grabbed her. I don't know what he did to her. I couldn't see."

"Was he driving a car you could see?"

"Yes, one of those dark European models. I had to hustle down to the stop sign and catch him after he left the alley. Black, I think. I got a partial plate." She gave

166

him the numbers.

"Okay, Letty, I'm coming now and bringing help. You stay put, okay, in case we have more questions."

"Will do, dear."

Trying to ignore the clutch of fear for Dayle's safety, he grabbed Sanchez. Pausing at the lieutenant's door to apprise him of the situation on the way out, he asked to borrow Seth Parker. Luckily, he was still in the precinct. Porter said he'd notify Dayle's boss about what had happened and marshal more officers to help search. On the way to the brownstone, Sanchez called in an all-points' bulletin on the car's partial plate and a "be on the lookout" advisory or BOLO on Christopher.

"I don't understand," he said to Sanchez. "She said she would stay put. Why would she leave her office when she knew it wasn't safe?"

"Knowing her, she's worried about what she's bringing to your doorstep."

He hadn't considered that. Sanchez was likely correct, but he wished he could shake some sense into his lover. Protecting her was a job he'd signed up for and wanted to keep.

Just as they screeched to a stop at the brownstone, Dayle's boss called. They had found the threatening note she had left open on her desk. It infuriated him that Christopher had used her fears about protecting him to manipulate her.

A search of the house and her cases told them nothing. They stopped and spoke to Letty, but she had nothing to add. She showed them how she'd followed their path with her binoculars and seen the car that sped away.

A warrant allowed another team to check

Christopher's apartment, but they'd found nothing except dozens of pictures of Dayle, both old and new, spread on a table. Frustration made his shoulders clench. "With his money, he could take her anywhere, even out of the country."

Sanchez looked at Seth and they both nodded, admitting the unspoken truth. If they didn't find a clue, he might kill her before they could figure it out.

****

When Dayle woke, her head throbbed with pain and she struggled to focus, bleary-eyed. The first thing she saw was the metal cuffs on her wrists. Another set were linked through them and fastened to the post of the makeshift bed she lay on. *What the hell! Where am I?*

"Oh, darling, you're awake." Ignoring the pain in her joints, she turned and saw Christopher sprawled in a nearby, striped lounge chair. He had a martini glass in his hand. Taking a sip, he set it down on the cheap, plastic table next to him. She looked around at the small rectangular building. The bare walls and one tiny window didn't provide any clues about where they were.

He walked towards her as his eyes traveled down her body. Without warning, he reached down and ripped the buttons on her blouse as he yanked it open. She heard one ping off the floor as the others went flying. Pulling a knife out of his pocket, he cut the rest off her quaking body. His actions stripped her down to her plain white bra. After that, he yanked off her slacks, revealing her panties, leaving her feeling vulnerable and exposed. "I must say, your taste in undergarments never improved, did it. I can remedy that."

She kept it blunt. "Let me go," she said through clenched teeth.

"Now, why in heavens would I do that? I would hardly go to all this trouble for nothing." He rubbed his hands together, a manic glee painting his face. "I have you here, where you belong, to use at my leisure. All your shenanigans were for naught. We could have saved a lot of time and trouble if you'd just done what you're told in the first place."

"You have no right to give me commands." Frantic for any clue about where they were, she noticed something odd about his shoes. Traces of a golden sediment trailed off each one. *Sand.* Were they at the beach?

He laughed, the edgy sound of it running chills down her back. "You still believe that given your current situation? That's hysterical." Standing, he came to the bedside, running two fingers down her legs. "I think the first order of business is to send a little hint of things to come to your beau." He lifted his phone, clearly recording her. When he changed position to point it at her face, she mouthed the word "beach," trying to make it subtle enough Christopher wouldn't notice.

Having her favorite cop understand might be her only hope.

****

Elijah and Sanchez had just returned to the office when the message from Christopher came through on his cell phone. He sucked in a breath, watching it, then called his partner and Seth over. Seeing her still alive gave him hope, but the sight of her shackled was almost too much to bear. It was too similar to what had happened to her last year. Could she survive such trauma twice?

"She's saying something." Sanchez pointed. "Watch her mouth when he does a close up on her face."

They took turns staring at it. Seth turned to him, "Is she saying bitch?"

They all tried to decipher it, watching it over and over. Elijah looked up. "Beach. I think she's saying beach." He ran a hand through his hair. "That's good. It narrows it down. It has to be either Staten Island or Long Island. He hasn't had time to get anywhere else."

"Jeez, Elijah, she's being held somewhere inside. That's thousands of possibilities."

"Maybe, maybe not. Do a deep dive on him. Where is his family from? I'd lay good money on it being Long Island. He's a pampered, rich boy, right? He would think that Staten Island too far beneath his standards."

"Okay," Sanchez agreed, slipping into her chair, firing up her computer. "I'll take care of that. You guys keep looking at that recording. See if you find anything else that might help."

"He might have chosen Staten Island to throw us off the scent," Seth suggested.

Elijah shook his head. "Old habits die hard. I honestly don't think he could force himself to go there."

****

"You bitch." Christopher stalked over to the bed and threw himself down on her again. "You will damn well respond to me!" Licking his way up her neck, he bit her ear. Still, she lay as stiff as a board, refusing to respond in any way. She knew he wanted her to fight. It fed his sickness, his fixation at controlling her. Her only hope lay in pretending to be totally unaffected by every move he made.

He groped her breast hard, twisting the nipple painfully. She concentrated on her breathing to keep calm, slow breaths in and out. "Don't you ignore me," he shrieked, jerking her face to stare into her eyes. He looked like the devil incarnate, his eyes ablaze with hate.

She said nothing, envisioning Elijah's face for comfort. Thinking all the calming phrases from her former yoga class, she reached for solace.

Christopher leapt off the bed, storming to the door and exiting. It slammed shut behind him. She had no idea where he headed, but she knew she was running out of time to escape. The night had been a constant replay of the same scene over and over again. He couldn't get sexually excited if she failed to respond. It was her only card to play. Soon, though, it was likely he'd give up and just kill her to end their toxic twosome.

But she'd thought of one long shot that might help her. She twisted painfully now to carry out her experiment. Her injury from last year made her hand less flexible. If she could access the metal underwire in her bra, the end might be tiny enough to slide inside and unlock her cuffs. If she could get free, she had an idea that might work even if she couldn't get out the padlocked door.

Twisting and turning, she managed to use a fingernail to shred a tiny piece of her bra at the bottom seam. It seemed to take forever, but, finally, a tiny seam opened. Feeling the end of the wire with one finger, she began to tug on it with her nails, hope blossoming in her chest. It felt like running a marathon as she tugged it over and over, panting with effort. One inch became two, then three. Finally, she yanked it loose.

Tears fell, and she brushed them away. *No time for crying.* Her blurry eyes strained to focus. Again and again, she poked the end into the tiny opening. The scraping sound taunted her until she thought go mad.

Click. The sound failed to register until she felt the cuff open. With no idea about how much time had passed, she started to panic. What if he came back too soon?

Dayle thought about Elijah, and it calmed her. She had to return to him. Failure wasn't in her vocabulary any more. With her free hand, she started to work on the second cuff. It opened almost immediately. Whispering a cheer, she scrambled up from the bed, her stiff muscles groaning, to carry out her plan.

****

The list of beaches on Long Island was daunting. Elijah called for official assistance which they needed because the locals knew the area so well. The nearby precincts sent teams of officers out to check each beach, starting with the largest.

He and Sanchez felt so frustrated that they began the drive there, leaving others to continue working at the office and calling with updates. All hands were on deck when the crime involved someone they worked with all the time, especially someone involved with one of them.

Roaring down the highway in their car, Sanchez looked at maps to familiarize herself with the lay of the land. Elijah drove as fast as he safely could toward where they prayed they would find Dayle in one piece and still breathing.

****

Dayle knew she couldn't fit through the single, tiny window, but she could make it look as if she had. She smashed the glass away by using the heel of her shoe, cutting her one hand by accident. Smearing some of the resulting blood on the edge of the glass added to the believability factor. Next, she gathered her torn blouse from the floor and left a shred of it attached to the window frame. She shrugged into what remained of it on and added her pants. That done, she paused to send a heartfelt prayer to whatever entity was listening and then stood on the bed. She never thought she'd thank any God for being a high school gymnast. Reaching up on her tiptoes, she grabbed the wood overhead and pulled up, then heaved herself onto the thick, wooden rafters above the wobbly bed. She didn't know how long she would have to hide there, but she would fight to the very end.

Wiggling into the very center of the thickest one, she lay there, praying her straining heart would quiet. For once, she thanked family genes for her skinny build and hoped she could stay truly hidden from view.

Waiting for what seemed like interminable hours, but was likely only minutes, she heard him return. The scrape of the lock was followed by an opening creak of the door. She heard two faltering steps as he stepped inside. "Godammit," he roared, staring at the empty bed before vaulting to stand by the tiny window and looking out.

Please don't look up. Please don't look up.

As if she'd scripted the scene, he raced to the door

and leapt out. From a flash through the window, she knew he'd headed to the right. Heart pounding, she forced herself to wait three or four minutes to make sure he didn't return at once. When only the sound of seagulls continued, she lowered herself to the bed, her hands clinging until she could drop. The mattress dipped to one side at her weight, and she scrambled off. Scurrying to the door, she looked out, first in one direction, then the other. The direction he'd headed in had scores of people within eyesight. She could see him in the distance, scanning back and forth.

His assumption that she'd head toward people wasted his precious time. Filling her lungs with air, she began to run, her feet sliding in the sand, in the opposite direction towards the dunes. All she desperately needed was one devoted nature lover with a phone.

Chapter Sixteen

As Elijah and Sanchez raced towards Long Island, the cop in charge of the search teams continued radioing in updates. His words kept breaking up, probably because of the location. Suddenly, the background noise doubled. The cacophony of sound was impossible to penetrate. Sanchez played with the radio to try and get better reception, but maybe they were too far away. It sounded like they were questioning a man who knew something, then they heard "...been found in the sand dune portion of the beach." Fear pounded like a hammer in Elijah's head. "Ask them to repeat transmission."

She tried to no avail, her strained gaze meeting his. The searchers had begun with the largest beach and then moved down in size. They were currently working the fourth beach they'd tried. It was still eight miles away. As he pressed harder on the accelerator, he tried to breathe evenly and not pass out. Anybody who worked beach areas knew the dunes were a terrific place to hide things.

Dead things.

****

A solitary man stood on the outer banks of the dunes, silhouetted against the brilliant sky. Dayle stumbled towards him, sobbing, as she held her blouse

175

together with one hand. "Please...I need help." Hurrying towards her, as much as the shifting sands allowed, he took her arm to steady her. He looked to be at least seventy with thinning gray hair and lined skin.

"Are you all right?" he asked, concern narrowing his eyes. "Did someone hurt you?"

"I need to call the police," she panted. "Have you got a phone?"

"No, but I have the next best thing." He pulled a walkie-talkie from his pocket. "We can call my buddy, Al, and he can relay a message to the local cops."

For once, luck was on her side. They got connected at once and she dictated a detailed message. Her savior's eyes got rounder by the second as he listened to her story. When Al assured them that help was on the way, he turned his unit off. "Did you see which way your ex-husband headed?" he asked, his nervous eyes darting back and forth.

"It's okay. He went the other way. That's why I took my chances on finding someone over here." She patted his arm to reassure him. "What's your name?"

"Ernest Hill."

"Well, Mr. Hill, my boyfriend's a detective. He's going to be thrilled I found you." Slumping to the ground to catch her breath, she leaned against his leg for support. After handing her his water bottle, he stood guard, a metal detector his only weapon. She drank, the still-cool liquid soothing her parched throat. Fifteen endless minutes later, four cops fought their way over the hills to her. They told her a host of other officers were combing the surrounding beaches for Christopher. She told him where she'd last seen him, then she, the police and Mr. Hill walked slowly to the gathering station for the search. They offered to carry her, but adrenaline continued to fuel her needs. By the time they got to the site, the area was teeming with onlookers as well as police, medics, and reporters. The latter screamed her name in a ragged chorus as she and the others made their way to the ambulance. She gratefully took a seat as the emergency technicians examined her. "Can you call Detective Black?" she asked. "He'll be sick with worry."

"I'll take care of it," one officer said. "In the meantime, let them check you out."

****

Arriving at the beach, Elijah shoved the car into park, leaving it where it stood despite the protest of a nearby policemen. He even left Sanchez to her slower approach, desperate hope making him run. Weaving in and out of the official vehicles, his searching gaze found Dayle standing beside the ambulance and he almost collapsed to his knees in gratitude. "Dayle!" he shouted. Ten anxious, loping strides took him to her side. Their eyes met, and he clasped her against him.

She tried to smile despite her exhaustion. "Why does this keep happening to me? First a crazed killer, then a psychotic ex-husband. Isn't that more than my fair share?"

He couldn't seem to let go of her, his hands shaking. "They said they found you and I thought...I thought..."

"I'm so sorry, Elijah."

"There was a lot of interference. I thought they meant your body, not you."

"Didn't they call? An officer said he would."

"No." He heaved in a breath and struggled to calm

his galloping pulse. "How the hell did you escape?"

She told him what she'd done. "Remind me to do extra upper body workouts. Getting up onto the rafters was harder than I expected." She tried to cheer him, worried about his pale face.

"Clever, clever girl." He peered around at the bustling officers. "Did they find him?"

"Last we heard, he was sighted at the far end, but he was surrounded by a crowd, so they were planning how to approach."

Twenty minutes later, they heard a shot in the distance. Crowding forward, they saw a scuffle between two cops and their quarry a hundred yards away. As if in slow motion, they spied a gun in Christopher's hand and heard someone shout a warning. "Down," a voice yelled and they saw the second cop raise his gun and shoot their suspect as the first cop hit the dirt. The shot hit center mass, an impressive feat since Christopher was only five feet away, too close to make aiming easy.

They waited, knowing that having more people around would just confuse things as their brothers and sisters in blue swarmed around the three men. After an interminable wait, the unit on the nearest officer to them crackled. He listened intently, then came striding over. "They got him. He made a grab for one officer's gun, but the second shot him. He's dead."

At their relieved collective gasp, he smiled. "The units are up here, so you can watch the ending if you wish. After that, we'll need a statement." He waved them forward. After a wait, they saw the body carried through the sand towards the waiting ambulance. They watched as press members surged forward, cameras raised, only to be contained by a barricade.

Turning to the cop who'd stayed with them, she read his badge. "Thank you so much for your assistance, Officer Dunlap. We appreciate your help. I hope you convey that to everyone involved."

"Yes, ma'am. It will be my pleasure." He leaned closer, lowering his voice. "It's nice to have a happy ending for a change."

She knew Christopher's family would hate to hear that sentiment, but only police understood how stalking victims suffer. She appreciated the show of support.

Taking a moment to introduce Elijah to her savior, Ernest, she watched as one of the patrolmen hustled him away to give his statement.

Elijah clasped her hand. "Let's head to the local precinct so we can get your victim's statement filled out and go home." They were shepherded away from the scene and travelled in a convoy that included news crews, whom they ignored.

Sanchez finally got her chance to contribute as they drove. "Your ex sure knew how to out on a show, didn't he? One of the guys said the first thing he said was, 'Do you know who I am?' " She snorted a laugh. "That's what all the rich dudes try, right, Elijah?"

"That's true." Seeing that the press had caught up to them, he hurried them inside the doors. The sooner they got started on the reports, the sooner they could go home.

Hours later, they dropped by their precinct to fill everyone in on what happened. After that, they drove Sanchez home and headed to their place. "You know, this has been a hell of a year," Dayle said, her mind trying to drink it all in.

He chuckled. "You got a new job, a new place to

live, got kidnapped by both a serial killer and a demonic ex-husband. Add in a new lover, and I think you're due for a restful year."

Leaning over, she squeezed his hand. "Not to get sickeningly romantic, but finding you makes everything else worthwhile."

He smiled and helped her out of the car. "I'm glad you think so, but I'm ready for a quiet night at home."

Home, she thought. That sounded awfully good to her.

They spent the next two days dealing with the fallout from the kidnapping. In order to quiet the press, they gave one sanctioned interview with Pamela to share what had happened, then asked for time to adjust and get back to their normal, busy lives.

After work, hours were spent preparing for Dayle's parents' visit. The guest room was prepared with fresh linens and a bouquet of roses for her mother. Elijah felt a little nervous about meeting them, but if they were anything like Dayle, it would be easy.

As they finished up, he looked at her fussing over the bed linens. "I love you, you know."

Looking up, she beamed. "I love you, too, Elijah." She moved across to his side of the bed and kissed him. The last-minute tidying could wait until the morning.

The timing of Dayle's parents' visit couldn't have been more timely. On Saturday morning, all he could think after Dayle's latest incident was how lucky it was that her parents hadn't been here at the time. It would have terrified them. Now, he and Dayle waited patiently at the airport for them to disembark from their plane. She had told them on the phone she fell and tripped, so they wouldn't freak out when they saw the bruises on her face and arms. He would tell them the truth later when they'd had time to settle in after their flight.

"There they are." She gestured to a couple near the back of the oncoming crowd. The first thing that surprised him was her mother's height. She was short, maybe five-foot-four as compared to Dayle's five-ten. Obviously, her height had come from her father's side. Since her real father had abandoned them, his name wouldn't come up any time soon. Her mom had short, dark hair threaded with gray, styled in a chic bob. Dayle' stepfather was maybe five-eleven with short gray hair and black framed glasses. He caught sight of Dayle's waving hand first and shepherded his wife across the wide aisle to them. He stood back as Dayle hugged both of them, then did the introductions. "Call me Debby," her mother said, giving him a hug. "And he's Mike."

Welcoming them, he led the way to the luggage carousel, then out to where a town car waited. "Oh, my, is this for us?" Debby asked.

"Yes, parking and traffic can be awful here. This is an easier option." He helped the driver load their cases. Seeing they were all safely seated, he climbed in the front passenger seat. The drive home took thirty minutes, moving steadily through congested streets. He let the ladies talk, only answering if they asked him a question. When the driver stopped in front of his brownstone, Debby's mouth gaped. "Oh, this is lovely. I had no idea what to expect."

Mike looked amused. "She'll want a tour, you know," he said as he climbed out. "She loves to see how other people live. Watches those decorating shows on television all the time." The men dealt with the luggage as the women went inside. When everyone was safely closed into the house, he and Mike carried the bags upstairs. When they returned, Debby oohed and ahhed over the furniture. "Oh, Elijah, your parents had lovely taste."

"Thank you, Debby. Mom was pretty proud of all the elbow grease she put into each piece."

She gave an enthusiastic sniff. "We were going to take you all out for dinner, but I smell something delicious."

"Dayle made us a lovely meal," he replied. "Perhaps we can dine out tomorrow."

Tonight's cook waved them farther down the hall. "I just have to make the sauce, and we'll be ready to eat." Hustling into the kitchen, she began to putter.

"Why don't I take your parents and show them the garden out back?" He knew she wanted the meal to be perfect and that would allow her some space to finish final touches.

"That's a good idea," she replied. "It will be about fifteen minutes, and dinner will be ready." She ducked into the kitchen as he and her parents made their way to the back of the house.

That should be long enough for his private talk. He herded them out onto the patio and shut the door behind him. Nerves buzzed in his stomach and he wanted to get conversation over and done so his nerves could settle. Mike eyed him, a knowing look in his eye. "Did you want to talk to us, son?"

"Yes, sir." Looking intrigued at his words, Debby returned to his side.

Elijah took a deep breath and let it out. "Dayle moved in with me a few weeks ago. There are several reasons for that. The first and most important reason is that I love your daughter. I chose this first step because I wanted to reassure her that she would be safe with me." If the beaming smiles were a good indication, this was going well. "In the near future, I would like to ask her to be my wife. I'm hoping for your blessing."

They stared at each other, smiling, before Debby moved towards him and spoke. "I'm happy to give you my enthusiastic support, Elijah. In our phone calls and, now, in person, she seems happier than she's been in years. I know it's largely because of you." Tears puddled at the corner of her eyes as she hugged him. Mike shook his hand.

"Thank you for your blessing. That's important to me. I wish my own parents were here to help us celebrate." He cleared his throat. "I think there's also something that you need to be aware of, although the problem has been dealt with." He told them about Christopher and his attack on Dayle, adding the final outcome.

"Why didn't she tell me?" Debby wrung her hands. "We thought he was still in jail."

"He got out early on good behavior, if you can believe that. I'm sure the people who made that decision are embarrassed and regretting their choice. This just happened three days ago. She fibbed for the short term because she didn't want you to panic when you saw her bruises."

"I hate him," she muttered. "I would have killed him myself, given the chance. He made their married life a misery, almost killed her, and that still wasn't enough for him."

He loved that she, at least, had two staunch

defenders who'd helped her pick up the pieces. Now, though, they could stand in line with him to support her. "The most important thing is that she's free of him now."

"Oh, thank you, Elijah. I guess you should never cheer the death of anyone, but hell is where he belongs."

"Your daughter is an amazing person. She saved herself, by using her skills. And you can be sure I'll protect her from this day forward."

She smiled, clasping her hands together. "You really do love her, don't you?"

"Yes, Debby, I certainly do. She's everything I ever wanted—smart and independent. She's kind and loving, too. That's a perfect combination for me."

As if the scene had been choreographed, a minute later, Dayle opened the door and called, "Time for dinner." They hurried inside. Sitting down to the table to eat together reminded him of his own parents and he smiled. On the platter, a sumptuous pork roast was cradled by whipped potatoes and broiled carrots. For dessert, she'd made a flourless chocolate cake with raspberries.

Dayle's meal was fabulous, and she blushed at all the compliments that came her way. "I think you were inspired by this beautiful kitchen," her mother said, winking. "That's the best meal I've eaten in ages."

Late that night, his lover lay curled in his arms where she belonged. Suddenly, she chuckled.

"What's so funny?"

She lowered her voice to a whisper. "Mom pulled me into a corner and asked if our relations were satisfying."

He choked out a laugh. "Your mom asked you about sex?"

"Yes."

"What did you say?"

She winked at him. "I told her that I probably won't have to go to the gym anymore because I'm doing a lot of heavy lifting at home."

They laughed, trying to keep their voices down so they didn't disturb them. "What did she reply?" he asked.

"She said, and I quote, 'He looks like he could carry you a mile or two.' " Laughing, they went to sleep.

By the time Debby and Mike went home four days later, Elijah realized he'd lucked out again. Dayle's parents had welcomed him into the family and made him feel comfortable in their midst. When he'd mentioned his difficult work hours and environment, Debby said, "No one gets any guarantees and I know you'll always be careful and protect our girl." Not everyone would think that way.

Chapter Seventeen

Three months later

Sanchez woke around midnight either from Ray's shuddering snores or just the fact that, no matter how she lay, some body part jabbed into her. She had ten days to go until her due date, and she hadn't managed a decent night's sleep in weeks. Grabbing ahold of the side of the mattress, she hauled herself to a sitting position, her legs dangling over the side of the bed. A damn crane would be needed if she didn't cough this baby out soon.

Standing carefully, she waited until she got her balance, then waddled towards the kitchen. A chocolate ice cream taco with caramel sauce had worked to settle her last night. She was willing to give it another shot. Halfway there, she sucked in a deep breath. These false contractions were driving her up the wall. Leaning against a doorframe for a minute, she felt a strange whoosh, followed by a dripping sound. Her feet were wet. *What the hell!*

Her predicament became clear as her brain finally got in gear. "Ray! Wake up," she shouted, trying to make herself heard over his racket. When her call didn't immediately elicit a response, she swore and turned to toddle back in his direction, one hand against the wall for safety. She hollered again.

"What...babe, where are you?" She heard his big feet hit the floor.

"Hallway."

A few bounding steps and he stuck his head out the bedroom door. "You okay?"

"Well, have a look at the puddle on the floor and you tell me."

In a stupor, his hair standing straight up, he stared, bug-eyed, at the evidence beside her. "Mother of God," he said. "It's too early."

She sighed. "Well, apparently baby didn't get the message. It's fine. Grab my coat and bag. Let's head for the hospital."

"What do we need?" he asked, his eyes panicking.

"Pants and t-shirt for you, jacket for me, hospital bag and keys. Now, get movin'."

She waited for him in the hall, swearing and holding her aching belly.

****

The shrill peal of the phone rang just before midnight, soon after Elijah and Dayle went to bed. Groaning, he reached for the phone, then suddenly realized it was Sanchez's ringtone. He swiped the button to answer, pushing the pursuit of sleep from his mind. "You okay?" he asked.

"It's Ray. It's baby time. Can you meet us at the hospital?" Excitement made him terse.

"Yup. Are you calm enough to drive?"

"Yeah, man, just meet us there."

They yanked on clothes, chuckling in anticipation. "She's going to be a handful," Dayle commented, reaching out to grab his arm. "I hope the nurses are ready for it." Jogging down the stairs, they barely remembered to lock the door behind them. They jumped into the car and hurried along the quiet streets to the hospital. At least parking was easier at that time of night. Inquiring how to find the labor and delivery department required a stop at the front desk, then they hurriedly followed directions down brightly lit halls.

As they headed for the hard, plastic seats in the waiting area, they heard a shouted string of curses in Spanish, the female voice a familiar companion. "We're in the right place," Elijah confirmed with a laugh.

She looked at the nearly empty chairs and said, "I'm surprised the rest of the family aren't here. There should be hordes of them by now."

"Sanchez asked Ray not to call them until, as she put it, 'we can see the football helmet on the kid's head.'" His eyes twinkled. "She was worried she'd have thirty people staring at what she calls her aging babymaker."

"Does she know we're here?"

He nodded. "I just texted Ray."

After a few minutes, the father-to-be stuck his head around the corner. "Hey, she wants to see you two. We still got a while to wait."

They followed him into the room. Sanchez lay against the raised bed, her upper body surrounded by pillows. "Elijah," she barked, her voice sounding strained. "Tell this damn kid to go ahead and come, right now. He's in overtime."

"No, he's not." His gaze took in her worried eyes. "Now, you know he just wants to make an appearance to remember, just like his mom. He'll come when he's ready."

"What's he doin', getting' a friggin' suntan? If I'm ready for him and he's not here, then he's late."

He smiled. "Ten days early makes him really punctual for first babies. They can often be as much as two weeks late."

That prompted another heartfelt string of curses. "Don't even suggest such crap. He'd better not decide to stay in there." When they all laughed, she glared at each of them in turn. "It's his fault," she accused, gesturing to Ray who stood leaning against the wall, smiling. "He's so damn relaxed about everything and the kid inherited it. Now that we're here, he doesn't think there's any damn hurry to join us."

"I love you, baby," her husband said.

"Oh, shut up. Loving me is what got us into this mess," she muttered with something akin to disgust. She peered up at the men, swiping her hair out of her face. "You two take a walk for a few minutes. I want to talk to Dayle."

They figured they'd better do as they were told, unsure of how she might respond if they didn't. Leaving the room with Ray, he moved down the hall, both of them stopping to prop up the wall. "What's she talking to Dayle about or is it girl stuff we shouldn't even think about?"

Ray met his gaze, grinning. "She's asking her to be our kid's godmother."

That shocked him. "I would have thought she'd choose someone in your family."

"Well, we thought about that, but here's the thing. Whoever we pick in the family, it's going to cause an all-out war. Someone's feelings are bound to get hurt. But if we pick our best friends, no one can say anything, right?"

"I guess that's true."

"So, what do you say? Are you up to the other part of the job?"

A smile spread across his face. "I'd be honored." He felt touched beyond words and shook the other man's hand, then did the man hug, grasping one shoulder.

"Good, because we need some backup to help teach him right from wrong. And we picked a name, too."

"What did you pick? I didn't hear any girl names which I figured was a clue. Last time I heard, you were considering Geraldo. And I know she already nixed Diablo, thank God."

He coughed out a sputtering laugh. "She just said that to throw you off the track. We're going to name him Antonio after my grandfather. Antonio Elijah."

Elijah stared at his friend in disbelief. "Are you serious?"

"You bet your skinny, white ass I am. We wouldn't have it any other way."

As they were hugging, the nurse stuck her head around the corner. "I've called the doctor. I think it's go-time."

They hustled to the room together. When he and Dayle went to leave, Sanchez said, "Oh, hell, no. I need my team here. Just, for God's sake, stand up beside my head. You damn well don't need to see anything that'll scar you for life."

He went to the top of her bed and held hands with Dayle who beamed at him. The doctor arrived in the middle of a contraction. She snapped gloves on. "Let's get this show on the road."

Within a few minutes, Ray was coaching Sanchez. "Come on, Alvia, we're almost there."

"What we, you moron? Are you lying here, pushing, in this bed?" She bore down, panting. "And, damn it, you know I hate that name." After a moment's rest, the next contraction came.

"I see his head," the doctor coaxed. "This next time, push hard."

"What the hell do you think I'm doing? He feels like he's driving a damn dump truck through there." She groaned, her face collapsed in effort, her muscles straining.

"One more push. I've almost got his shoulders."

Sanchez's groan surged to a crescendo that rattled the windows. Ray's face beamed. "There's my boy," he murmured, tears dripping down his cheeks. "There's Antonio." A slight thud was heard as the doctor tapped the baby's back. She handed him to the nurses to clear his throat. A moment later, a shrill, earthy cry split the room. They watched as the nurses checked him and cleaned him off.

"I did it," Sanchez said, looking up at Dayle. The look of wonder on her face was priceless.

"You sure did. He's a handsome chunk, isn't he?"

"Bring him to me," she commanded, like a true Mexican Madonna. "I want to hold my son."

Ray waited until they checked and weighed him before cradling him in his arms. He moved to Sanchez's side. "Meet your boy, Momma." Gently, he passed him to lie in her arms.

Sanchez cradled him against her chest, her eyes bugging out in disbelief. She tucked a finger inside one tiny hand and looked up. "He's beautiful," she whispered, her voice cracking, then she burst into tears. "I can't believe he's ours," she sobbed.

Dayle stroked her hair. "I believe it. Look, he's tall, like Ray, and he has your gorgeous eyes."

Ray leaned over to kiss her. "He's almost as beautiful as my girl."

After Ray's phone call, members of the family started showing up at once, fellow officers not long after. A seemingly endless parade of visitors tramped through the room. Dayle took charge of organizing the flowers and gifts to help out. Their lieutenant came, Pamela with Seth, and too many others to count. Finally, they'd all been seen, and Sanchez was exhausted. The room looked like a gift store. The baby had fallen asleep and lay peacefully tucked into his mobile bed next to her, a blue cap covering his dark curls.

"It's time for us to go so you guys can get some sleep. Be sure to call if you need anything." Elijah cleared his throat. "I just wanted to tell you that we truly are a family, all of us. We've got cops and civilians, news reporters and lawyers, but, in the end, all that matters is we're here for each other, always." He reached out to take Dayle's hand. "And we'll be proud to take care of your boy as if he was our own."

Ray nodded, his eyes glassy with tears. "Thanks, you two. That means the world to us."

Sanchez waved Elijah over, beckoning him to lean down. He put his ear next to her mouth. "Time to marry that chick," she whispered.

Standing, he smiled, raising her hand to kiss the back of it. "I'm working on it." They left the room with one last look at the new family. He and Dayle both stayed quiet on the drive home. After he pulled in the driveway, they just sat for a moment. "It makes you think, doesn't it? How short life is and how important it is to make every moment count. It seems like yesterday when she swore she'd never get married."

"Yes." She sighed. "They looked so much in love with each other and that beautiful baby."

"I know." He reached over to squeeze her hand and contemplate how lucky he felt. "I can't believe how much my life has changed in the last eighteen months. I feel like my parents are looking down on us and smiling with approval. They would have loved you."

"That's such sweet thing to say."

"It's true." He released her hand, raising an eyebrow. "Want to go plan a wedding with me?"

"Well, to borrow a saying from Sanchez, do the best donuts have sprinkles? Hell, yes. And how did you know I'd want a low-stress proposal?"

"I can read you," he said, smiling. "What kind of wedding do you want?"

She pondered for a moment. "A quiet one, in our back yard, with a dozen friends and my parents."

"That sounds like it's right up my alley."

Cocking her head at him, she said, "You asked my parents for permission, didn't you?"

He flushed. "What can I say? I'm just an old-fashioned guy."

"You and me both, Elijah."

"And, Dayle?"

"Yes."

"As soon as possible, okay?"

"You've got it. Is three months or less okay?"

"Perfect."

Epilogue

Six weeks later, Elijah stood looking at the newly renovated family shelter, Dayle at his side. Now that it was finally finished, the two of them had joined Seth, Pamela, Ray, and Sanchez for a small celebration of their efforts. Baby Antonio was along for the ride, strapped to Ray's chest in a carrier.

They made the rounds with Sara, who beamed from ear to ear. The kitchen, along with its new seating plan and appliances, was complete. The sleep area had been outfitted by new bunk beds for the kids which made room for more families. Best of all was the new education area in what been an unused end of the common room.

They stood looking at the renovated area with pleasure. The cramped tables had been replaced with two huge couches and the television had a big screen so everyone could see. At the other end, four computers were placed on large desks. "I can't believe you found someone to donate the computers, Dayle." Sara touched her arm. "The kids are so excited about them. They even worked out a sharing schedule so everyone gets a chance to enjoy them."

"It's been our pleasure." After they finished their celebration tour, they stopped for cookies and soda before they headed out to lunch together.

"The kids look so much happier," Elijah said. "It's

great to see that. And, now, you can get started finding an assistant to make your job easier."

"Having more things for them to do gives their mothers a chance to get much-needed breaks. And an assistant will provide a break for me." Sara rubbed her hands together. "We really would have been lost without all of you. Not just the donations, but all of the volunteer hours, along with the friends you brought from your precinct."

Hugging her, Elijah said their goodbyes and they headed for the door. He paused, looking back for a moment, and his eyes settled on the sign over the common area door. It read "Cara's Corner." Seth had made the wooden art piece and hung it at his request.

A stranger might wonder why he would suggest a murderess's name being on such a happy place, but they hadn't known her convoluted history as he had. Inside her twisted mind had once lived a young woman who just wanted to survive her abuse. In the end, she had left a legacy that would save hundreds from the same fate. Her massive contribution to the end result meant her name deserved to be there. It was her legacy of hope.

Now that he had carried out the first stage of her plan to help others, he would stop visiting her grave every week. It was time to move on and continue promoting her cause along the way. He'd found a woman he loved, a career where he could make a difference and the best friends in the universe. He didn't need her money. He was already the richest man in the world.

"Are you coming?" Dayle stood inside the doorway, concern darkening her eyes.

He smiled as he joined her. grabbing her hand. "There's nowhere else I'd rather be." They hurried to catch up to the others.

A word about the author...

Dianne McCartney has been writing for eighteen years and has won sixty-three writing awards in contests across Texas and Oklahoma. She is a long-standing member of the Oklahoma Writers Federation, Inc. and a proud member of the Rose Rock Writers.
Website:
www.diannemccartney.com
Social Media Links:
https://twitter.com/authorDMcC
https://www.linkedin.com/in/dianne-mccartney-36a493161/
https://www.facebook.com/dianne.mccartney.3914/
https://www.instagram.com/diannemccartney1200